Uncharted

Book 1
Serendipity Adventure Romance

Anna Lowe

Contents

Other books in this series

Serendipity Adventure Romance

Off the Charts

Uncharted

Entangled

Windswept

Adrift

www.annalowebooks.com

Free Books

Get your free e-books now!

Sign up for my newsletter at *annalowebooks.com* to get three free books!

- *Desert Wolf*: Friend or Foe (Book 1.1 in the Twin Moon Ranch series)

- *Off the Charts* (the prequel to the Serendipity Adventure series)

- *Perfection* (the prequel to the Blue Moon Saloon series)

Chapter One

Julie rolled her Kawasaki to a stop, pulled out her passport, and held it out for inspection.

The border guard spent more time checking out her motorcycle — or possibly her ass, given the way he leaned right — than her passport. Eventually, he rifled through a few pages and handed it back. "Welcome to Belize."

"Gracias." She waved, tucked the passport away, and revved the bike down the road after a goodbye glance toward Guatemala. The six months she'd spent there were everything she'd hoped for, but it was time for new adventures. Like exploring out-of-the-way ruins just for fun, because she'd been immersed in archaeological research for so long, she'd almost forgotten to appreciate the beauty of Mayan architecture. Or heading into the rainforest to listen to howler monkeys. Maybe scuba dive on the rainbow reefs of Belize's Caribbean coast, if she could find a cheap enough deal.

Small, tame adventures, that's what she had in mind. Two weeks of fun as a reward for six months of sweaty field work before she headed home and buckled down on her thesis.

The bike hummed down the road, and she could picture the coast already. The kaleidoscope reefs, the pristine sand. Heck, she could practically smell the salt in the air, hear the sound of waves swishing over a beach.

Yes, she'd be there in no time. A couple of hours' joy ride, and she'd be kicking back in the shade of a palm on a Caribbean beach with a good book. That's how she'd start this little vacation. With peace. Solitude. Time to relax before she decided just which flavor of adventure to try next.

An ear-splitting screech filled the road behind her, and her eyes jumped to the sideview mirror.

A couple of jeeps came flying onto the bumpy tropical road behind her and started weaving in and out of cars, chasing someone. Someone in a hell of a lot of trouble, judging by the dust clouds those jeeps were kicking up. She put the blinker on to get out of the way. The jeeps were racing up behind her, getting frighteningly close, the engines roaring ever nearer.

She was about to pull over when she checked the mirror again — and did a double take.

The faces in the jeeps, the gesturing hands — they were all aimed at her.

So were the barrels of three or four machine guns.

She stared in the mirror so hard, she nearly rammed the flatbed truck ahead of her.

Those jeeps weren't chasing *someone*. They were chasing her.

Me?

The gears in her mind whirred, trying to come up with an explanation. Maybe they were after someone else. Maybe they were just waving her out of their way. That had to be it, right?

But the minute she slowed to pull over, they did too. And when she took off again in a panic, they followed suit. Lights flashing, tires squealing — the works.

Wind whipped at her face as she hunched over the handlebars and accelerated around the flatbed truck. What? How? Why were they after her? She hadn't done anything!

And yet there she was, speeding down the highway at breakneck speed, overtaking cars, mules, and fume-spewing buses. All the while, the two jeeps stuck to her like flies to a carcass — a fitting image, considering how close she came to some of the vehicles. Close enough to shatter her motorcycle's side mirror with a high-pitched crack against a truck loaded with squawking chickens. Close enough that she'd be lying, big-time, next time she called her mother to promise how careful she was being while traveling Latin America alone.

She could hear the conversation now.

"Have you been taking care of yourself, sweetheart?" her mother would ask.

"Um. . . yes." Apart from high-speed chases down crowded roads, maybe.

Racing away had been a mistake, for sure. Only the guilty fled, and she wasn't guilty of anything but the occasional jaywalking. She was the one who always stuck to the speed limit. The one who never left anything off her taxes, even back when she'd been earning money before going back for her master's degree. She was the one who carefully recorded every artifact she discovered, lest any of them fall into the wrong hands.

But trying to explain that to a band of gun-waving commandos in unmarked vehicles had zero appeal. And a single woman pulling over for five or six men on the side of a Central American highway? No way.

Vrooom! She revved the engine higher and peeled off across the oncoming lane.

Horns blared; she barely slotted between two speeding cars. Hunched low over the handlebars, she shot down a side track overhung with vines as the road behind her erupted with noise. Tires screeched against asphalt; a sickening metal-to-metal crunch signaled a collision. Julie didn't look back. She didn't need to. The whine of an engine said one of the two jeeps was still hot on her tail.

Who could be chasing her? Why? Those jeeps could be police, military, or mercenary. In Central America, it was hard to tell.

The road ahead branched. She swung a hard left and ended up careening through a winding hillside village. A man bent low under a load of firewood paused in midstep to gape.

"Watch out!" she hollered and clattered down an impossibly narrow lane. Mud splattered and the smell of cow dung filled her nostrils; the handlebars rattled under her arms.

A slack-jawed villager watched her speed by. Another waved his arms as he yelled for her to stop.

"*Alto!*" She barely heard him over the roaring engine, but the message was pretty clear. "*Alto!*"

Stop? Like hell, she was stopping now. She slalomed around a pothole and thundered on.

"Sorry!" She owed at least a dozen apologies by the time she shot out the other side of the village because she'd wiped out a laundry line, scattered a family of pigs, and excited a schoolyard of children as she whizzed past. But hell, it worked. The jeep chasing her must have gotten stuck somewhere along the way, because all she could hear now was the steady hum of the Kawasaki's engine.

That, and the thumping of her own heart. Jesus Christ. What had that been all about?

She asked herself the question again and again over the next two hours, flying down back roads to put extra distance between herself and the men in pursuit. It was only when the coast came into view that she relaxed her white-knuckled grip and pulled over to think.

If she hadn't done anything wrong, why were the police after her?

She squirmed, trying to settle her backpack more comfortably between her shoulder blades. The corner of something hard kept jutting into her back, and—

She froze.

The backpack. The box inside it.

The box she'd agreed to bring to Belize as a favor to the professor in charge of her last dig.

Oh my God.

All around her, jungle birds chirped, and it sounded like gossip and laughter aimed at her back. Julie, the numbskull. Julie, the naive.

"It's just some documents, together with a small gift," Professor Leeds had said when he'd asked her to take it with her. "I support an orphanage in Belize. Won't you be so kind as to deliver it for me?"

She swung the small backpack off her shoulders and into her lap then started burrowing frantically in it for the box. Fumbling with the brown paper wrapping. Prying a corner up. Peeking.

Going stiff all over when she realized what was inside.

Holy shit.

The professor's lie was as transparent as the turquoise water that stretched in ribbons of green and blue all the way to the Caribbean horizon. She hadn't been carrying a gift. She'd been smuggling.

No wonder she was being chased.

Chapter Two

After a long detour through fields, over a creaky wooden bridge, and down a meandering footpath, Julie rolled into the sleepy town of Santa Marta and made straight for her favorite seaside café. The calming sound of waves over a beach, the stunning pastel colors of the reefs, and a cool drink — those would help her make sense of things, right?

She'd never planned on coming back to Santa Marta, but it seemed as though instinct had guided her here. Misguided was more like it, because there were too many memories, too much heartache associated with the place. But at some point in that crazy morning, she'd stopped thinking and just followed her gut. And rather than hightailing it north to Mexico, she'd somehow ended up in the quiet Caribbean beach town she used to call her favorite place on earth.

She settled into a chair at the Coco Loco Café and took a deep breath. It had been a hell of a day, even by her standards.

She lifted her sun hat just enough to wipe the sweat from her brow then tugged it back down — low. The fewer people who noticed her, the better. She leaned back in the shade of the beachside café, watching the sunlight flicker through the swaying palms.

A hell of a day, and it was only eleven in the morning.

Yeah, she would definitely be more careful in what she wished for from now on. What happened to small adventures? Down time? That's what she'd had in mind.

Not *this*. Definitely not this.

She held the cool glass of her smoothie against her cheek for a moment before finding the straw with her lips. Maybe a cool sip of papaya and ice would slow down her runaway thoughts and make things seem normal again, because she'd left normal behind at the border.

She closed her eyes and pulled her hat lower, trying to tune out the tourist chitchat drifting over from the other tables.

"I swear there were more chickens on the roof of that bus than people inside."

"Yeah, the driver had great reflexes — with the horn! He barely touched the brakes, though."

"That's what I always say. You want adventure? Just ride a bus in Central America."

Adventure? Buses? If only they knew. That morning, she'd had it all. Her heart was still pounding in her chest, her arms shaking from jackhammering over so many bumps.

The floorboards of the café's terrace creaked as someone came closer, and a shadow blanketed her face. She could feel it, even with her eyes closed. Her nostrils flared at the scent. It was familiar, somehow.

Pleasing.

Masculine.

Close.

Her pulse spiked and her gut warmed as it dawned on her who it was.

Not him. Please, not him.

Hadn't she already been dragged through enough this morning? And now *this?*

"Julie," a quiet voice said. An all-too-familiar voice she'd once had close to her ear. Close to all kinds of body parts, actually.

Even with her eyes shut, she knew who it was. And opening her eyes only made things worse, because she couldn't pretend she was dreaming.

"You," she said, narrowing her eyes. Because it really was him.

Caramel brown eyes, soft and sincere. Chiseled cheeks and thin, accent-mark eyebrows that said he'd been worrying, wondering. Perfect white teeth behind perfect coral-pink lips flashed a thin smile that promised he remembered every hot night they'd spent together, every idyllic day in what had been the best week of her life.

Seth.

He plopped down in the seat across from her, looking penitent and pained. Half of her wanted to throw herself into his arms the way she had the first night they'd met; the other half wanted to fling her drink in his face.

"About that Friday," he began. From his tone, you would have thought *that Friday* was two days ago instead of two months. The Friday he'd walked out on her.

"The Friday you stood me up." She leveled the words right back at him.

He put his hands up like a guilty man. "I can explain."

"I bet you can."

"The weather changed."

She threw her head back and barked out a humorless laugh. "The weather. Right."

"Julie," he said, and it was a whisper. A plea.

And silly girl, she let down her guard and allowed herself to look into his eyes. Big mistake, because those eyes could seduce a woman in broad daylight. Those eyes and that earnest expression that said, *Trust me, I'm a good guy.* It was just like the day they met in a spot just down the road. She'd come to Belize for the week she had off from her excavation site in Guatemala and had barely settled into reading her book when Seth came ambling up to her. And just like that, she got lost in eyes that smiled at her — smiled like she was what he'd traveled all the way from North America to see. Like she was his destination. Like he saw a whole story ahead of them and couldn't wait to live it out with her in real time.

"Not even a note. Not even goodbye." God, she sounded bitter. But hell, she was. She'd given in the very night she met him in the first one-night stand of her life. Woken up the next morning wrapped around him and ended up spending most of the week that way. But when Friday rolled around...

"I thought we had..." She trailed off, not ready to say the rest. *I thought we had something special.*

I thought so, too, his eyes said like he'd read her mind.

She shook her head. Two months, and damn it, he only looked more delicious. His black-brown hair was long enough to curl around his ears now, his tan an even deeper shade of bronze. When she first met him, he'd still carried the last vestiges of corporate New York with him: the furrowed brow, the restless fingers, the hurried walk. But now, the watch was gone, his shirt untucked, his jaw unshaven. He was more buccaneer than weekend sailor now — and Christ, she'd better watch out.

The waitress cantered over far more quickly than she had for Julie and fluttered her eyelashes at Seth. "Can I get you a drink?"

"Yes," he said.

"No!" Julie barked.

The waitress looked between them, holding her tray up like a shield. "Maybe I'll give you a minute."

Right, a minute. Like that would help.

"Julie." Seth picked up again once the waitress was gone.

She put a hand up to halt him before his soft tones could melt her all over again. So what if he kissed like a pirate just back in to port? This time, she'd be stronger, smarter. This time, she'd send him on his way.

"Seth," she started, getting ready to do just that. "Don't even—"

She didn't finish, because the road behind him sounded with the squeal of brakes, the creak and subsequent slamming of doors. Three scrappy mutts that had been snoozing beside the street scattered as a half-dozen men in khaki uniforms jumped out of two jeeps and scanned the street.

Shit.

Her eyes jumped to Seth, to the men on the road, then back to Seth. Her heart started pounding again, and her mind spun. Get away! Get away!

But how? Where?

Her gaze swung to where she'd left her motorcycle then over to Seth, and seconds slowed as her stomach bucked in a series of crazy little flips.

It was Seth or the band of death-dealing thugs closing in from over there. Not really much of a choice, because even a heartbreaker was the lesser of those two evils.

"Can you drive a motorcycle?" she asked, holding her breath.

He blinked. "What?"

"Can you drive a motorcycle?"

Chapter Three

Could he drive a motorcycle?

Seth stared at Julie, trying to articulate all the emotions jumping from his heart into his throat. Maybe even hoping for her to throw herself into his arms. But no, that wouldn't have been Julie: Indiana Jones with two X chromosomes. Not that she had any of the props: no hat, no whip, no leather jacket. Just the glint in her eye, the ready posture, the stories to tell.

"Uh. . . yeah, I can ride a bike," he managed, wondering why it mattered. Wondering what she was doing here. He'd been through town so many times looking for her. And now — his last chance before sailing south to Panama — Julie was there. If that wasn't fate, what was?

Except she didn't seem too willing to give fate a chance, and he was screwing everything up. But how could a man think straight when everything inside him was on fire?

He scraped his fingers through his hair and scrubbed his palms over his cheeks. Because it really was her. Julie with her sea-green eyes and kissable lips and pointed, pixie chin. Julie with the habit of sucking in her cheeks and tugging on her sandy brown ponytail before saying whatever was on her mind. Julie melted him, every time. Tough as nails on the outside, soft as a kitten inside. He knew; he'd seen her kick a ball around with the local kids and save food scraps for scraggly alley mutts. Seen her look at the wide horizon and quietly wish.

But there was something vulnerable about her now, and he ached to know what it was. The first moment she looked up at him, her eyes had flashed with more than just anger, and he wanted to know what that was, too.

And yet all he had come up with was *I can explain.*

"Then take it. Take the bike." She motioned down the road with one hand and dug into her pocket with the other. "Drive around the block. Meet me around the back."

"Um—"

Her eyes had been shooting daggers at him, but now they were fixed over his shoulder. Wide in surprise — or was that fear? Seth spun around and saw half a dozen fatigue-clad solider-types piling out of two jeeps. By the time he turned back to Julie, she had the brim of her hat pulled so low, he could barely see her chin. What was going on?

"Take the bike. Now!" she barked and shot a ring of keys over to him. They made a scratchy metallic sound as they zipped across the Formica tabletop and nipped his palm.

"Get it." A twitch of her shoulder told him which direction the motorcycle was parked. "Meet me around the back." She pushed away from the table so fast, her chair fell back, but quick as a panther, she shot out a hand and caught it.

"Julie—"

That was all he'd managed before she swung her backpack to her shoulder and took off.

"Just go! Hurry!"

"Jul—" he protested, but she was already gone.

Chapter Four

Seth blinked in her wake. Julie's first two steps were a hurried walk. The next two were a jog, and then she was sprinting up the crooked path that ran between the café and the wall of the neighboring property.

"Julie?"

He'd been out that way once or twice. There was nothing back there but a squat toilet and a demon of a dog on a chain that was too long for comfort by about four links. The path ended in a cement-block wall topped with shards of broken glass that poked up like the toothy jaws of a shark. Where did she think she was going?

"*Alto!* Stop!"

Shouts rang out and footsteps pounded through the café. Seth spun to see four soldier-cops — big ones — taking up the chase.

Chasing Julie? Jesus, what had she done?

The dog out back started barking, and Seth pictured Julie staring desperately up that too-high wall.

"Watch it, man!" one of the backpackers yelped.

The first cop dodged the man's chair then ducked under a fluttering red-and-blue blur — the café's pet toucan, perched on a trapeze. A second man was right on his heels, holding a hand to the bulge in his jacket as if cushioning something inside. A gun?

"Hey! Stop!" The waitress protested the intrusion in the same high-pitched squawks as the wildly flapping toucan, but the men shoved right past her, sending a tray of pink-hued smoothies in tall glasses with green-and-yellow striped straws sailing through the air in a moment that played out in a weird slow-motion way in Seth's mind.

Julie. Running.

Men. Chasing. Men with guns.

The smoothie glasses shattered on the hard floor, and something primal inside him roared. If he could have ripped out of his skin and turned into a grizzly, he would have, there and then.

Stop them! Save her!

But Julie's words were still front and center in his mind. *Get the bike!*

Only she could say those words on the way to running full tilt into a dead end.

If he did as she said, he'd probably arrive just in time to see a handcuffed Julie being wrestled into a jeep, kicking and biting and cussing the men out all the way to some awful fate.

If he didn't do as she said…she'd still be wrestled into a jeep, kicking and biting and cussing *him* out on her way to some awful fate.

He jumped to his feet, pushing his chair into the aisle to trip up the first man.

"Oi!" the man cried, going down hard.

Seth's rising shoulder met the second man's chin. There was a distinct "Ooof!" as the man reeled away.

"Hey, man!" Seth said, putting his hands up in feigned surprise. "Watch out!"

The man growled and clawed past. *Bump* — Seth detoured into the third guy and, *whoops* — tripped up a fourth. Apart from cursing, they all scurried onward, intent on their prey.

There was an explosion of growls and cries as the men ran out of sight and encountered the snarling dog. Cerberus — that's what Julie called him. She used to butter the mutt up with food scraps and that special doggie-magic voice she used on animals, little kids, and slow-thinking bartenders. So she might just have a moment's reprieve.

Still, there was that wall topped with a jagged row of broken glass — the third-world version of barbed wire. How would she get over that?

But if there was one thing Seth had learned about Julie in the week they'd spent in each other's arms — other than she had silky skin and a sweet smile and legs that could play tricks on a man's mind — was that the impossible was possible. That, and the fact that Julie hated being second-guessed. So he dashed through the pandemonium of the café and wheeled right, sprinting down the block. He spotted the bike behind a half-collapsed wall, pushed it onto the street, and hopped on. When he fired it up, his calf squeezed against something cool and smooth — the steel of a machete she kept strapped to the old leather saddlebag on the right side of the bike.

He roared around the corner, turned again to square the block, and came up parallel with the back of the café. And damned if Julie wasn't already there, running toward him at full steam. Before he came to a stop, she swung up behind him like a cowgirl and thumped him on the arm.

"Go! Go!" she yelled, grabbing his waist.

Chapter Five

Seth twisted the throttle so hard, the front tire nearly came off the ground. They raced down the alley, scattering the two cops who'd made it over the wall. A third was half-falling, half-jumping off the top, and the fourth was perched awkwardly atop it, holding his hand and screaming in pain.

Julie's hands squeezed his ribs. "Hit it! Go!"

"Jesus, Julie, what did you do?" he shouted over his shoulder.

"I didn't do anything!"

Something cracked in the alley and whizzed past his ear, and he ducked on instinct. "Holy shit!" Were the men really shooting? At them?

Julie leaned in and shouted. "Faster!" She'd hollered quite a few instructions in his ear, once upon a time, and he'd always been more than willing to oblige. But this was life-or-death, and he was one step ahead of her, accelerating toward the next corner to get out of the line of fire.

A second bullet whistled past his ear the exact instant that Julie blurted a curse and lurched, throwing the bike off-balance. She clutched his shirt. He stuck out his right foot and scraped the sole of his shoe along the dirt road, trying not to wipe out.

"Julie?"

She righted herself and tightened her grip around his waist.

"Are you okay?" He threw the words over his shoulder.

"I'm fine," she said, but her voice was unnaturally tight. "Go!"

He shifted his weight and took the corner at high speed. As soon as he did, his ears exploded with noise.

Beeeep!

For a split second, there was just that godawful noise and the sight of a metal grill barreling down on him — the front of a bus. A bus about to wipe him and his cowgirl into oblivion before he had a chance to say everything he needed to say to her. One of those wildly decorated Central American buses airbrushed in blazing colors, with red flames and a set of shark teeth painted around the hood.

He swerved at the last second, screaming inside. The bus shot past so close, he could feel the suck of air on his skin. A twist of the throttle took them through a cloud of blue exhaust and then into the clear.

The screech of bus brakes was still echoing in his mind as he gunned down the main street, heart hammering in his chest. He took the next left and rocketed down the coastal road with no clue where he was going, as long as it was away. Far away.

Julie's hand bumped his arm and pointed left. He saw blood first, because her hand was smeared with it, but she was pointing so insistently that he had to look up to a winding dirt lane that disappeared into a strip of jungle.

"There! Go that way!"

There was just enough space to cut in front of a lumbering truck in the oncoming lane. He flew up the lane, around a tight corner where thick vines hung low over the road, and stopped, killing the engine. Julie was stiff against his back, listening for any sound of pursuit. Her chest heaved with panting breaths, just like his. Like they'd been sprinting for their lives instead of riding her vintage Kawasaki.

Vintage. Part of him chuckled inside. He'd called the bike old once, and she'd taken it as a personal affront.

"Lucy is not old!"

"Lucy?"

"The bike. And the word is vintage, not old."

That was Julie; she had her pride. Bucketloads of it. That and a personality big enough to fill any inanimate objects around her with life.

Behind the curtain of trees, traffic rumbled by on the coastal highway. The noise rose as racing tires and a series of commanding beeps sped by. Every muscle in his body tensed until the jeeps swept past, and the pitch changed then faded as the space around him filled with the calls of aggravated forest birds.

Seth closed his eyes. They were safe. For the moment, at least.

Without thinking, he crossed an arm over his chest to grasp Julie's hand, still clutched at his shoulder. Something warm and sticky leaked onto his fingers. Julie's body was rock hard. He twisted in his seat.

"Hey, are you all right?"

"I'm fine," she said between gritted teeth. "Let's get out of here."

His eyes traced the blood to her shoulder.

"Christ, Julie!"

"It's not so bad."

"Man, what did you do?"

She thumped his ribs. "I didn't do anything! And why did you take so long?"

Only Julie would come up with a line like that at a time like this. If he wasn't still shaking, he might have laughed out loud.

"Okay, let's get out of here." Easy to say, but what to do? The jeeps wouldn't go far before they turned around and came back. Where could he take Julie to keep her safe?

His eyes swept right, and though he couldn't see through the strip of jungle, he could smell the salt of the sea that lay beyond. Could picture the vibrant stripes of blues and greens, the silvery horizon.

He turned back to Julie, who was still panting and wild-eyed. She was so close, his heart stuttered and thunked, and he couldn't help but cup her cheek. They were eye to eye, body to body.

He'd tried so hard to forget this — this pull that set in every time Julie got close. But it felt so right to have her there, even if the circumstances were all wrong.

He dragged his eyes away and straightened to kick the engine back to life.

"Where to?" Her voice wavered just the way her gaze had when he'd touched her.

"We'll head back to town and hide the bike," he said, twisting once more on the seat.

"They'll find it. They'll find us."

Us. He liked the sound of that.

"Not if we hide it well." He risked a cocky grin. "And not if we head where they won't expect us to go."

She looked at him, her green eyes questioning.

"The boat. We get on the boat and sail away."

She stared at him like he'd just offered her a ride on a magic carpet. "The boat?" she murmured. "Your boat? *Serendipity?*"

His chest went all warm. "Yeah, *Serendipity.* Let's go."

Chapter Six

"Julie?"

She blinked three or four times until the world came back into focus. There was a hand reaching out from overhead, a voice calling her name. The curved stern of a sailboat filled her vision, and the sea rocked beneath her. The voice came from somewhere higher up, past the metal piping that formed a rail at the back of the boat and above the curved letters that spelled the sailboat's name: *SERENDIPITY.*

"You okay?" Seth asked from behind.

She blinked again, trying to break through the fog that had taken over her thoughts.

"Come on, Tobin, help her up," Seth said.

Seth's strong, steady presence must have let her slip into a daze, because she was still sitting in the dinghy, trying to process everything that happened. Being chased. Escaping on the motorcycle. Being grazed by a bullet, if not directly hit. Ditching the bike then hurrying to the dinghy to get to Seth's boat, where his brother waited.

Tobin. That was Seth's brother's name. The funny one with the thousand-watt smile and cheeky grin. The kind who would fit right into a Chippendales lineup or the pages of a magazine. She'd met the brother about thirty seconds before meeting Seth, because Tobin was the one who'd immediately come on to her in a bar all those weeks ago. She'd brushed Tobin right off, uninterested, and Seth came over to apologize for his brother. She was going to dismiss Seth just as quickly, but somehow, she got stuck on those eyes, that quiet voice.

She winced as Tobin hauled her up by her bad arm.

"Jesus, what happened?"

She was wondering the same thing.

Seth left her in the cockpit, wrapped in a beach towel like a lost kitten while he and Tobin scurried around the boat, hurrying to weigh anchor. Funny how he'd always talked about inviting her aboard but this was her first time. He'd always had one excuse or another, most of them involving his brother. And anyway, they'd been having too good a time burning up the sheets in her beach bungalow to budge far. God, it hadn't taken much for her to fall for him. Seth, the New York business consultant turned sea adventurer. What had she been thinking?

Warmth seeped into her body as she remembered the way he'd tilt his head to listen to her — really listen. The way he'd slowly stroke the length of her arm with one finger. The way his gaze would go all intent like nothing on earth was more important to him than her.

Yeah, a girl could be forgiven for falling for a guy like that. But falling that hard and that fast… That part was hard to forgive. She was supposed to be tough. Independent. Strong.

"Secure the dinghy. I'll get the sail," Seth called to his brother.

Julie looked around, trying to get oriented. Until now, she'd only seen the boat from a distance, but even that was enough to impress her. Not so much by its fanciness, because it was a smallish, older sailboat, but in what it promised. Adventure. New horizons. Just thinking about it made her lungs expand. That sense of possibility.

But she'd let her imagination get ahead of itself. By day three of their week together, she'd been silently hoping that she could keep seeing Seth. Thinking she might be able to hook up with him somewhere along the coast when she wrapped up her research. Together, they could sail from island to island and—

Silly girl.

She dropped her chin to her chest and closed her eyes as Seth came through the cockpit once again. His hand touched her arm and she found those honey-brown eyes studying hers.

"You okay?" His voice was scratchy, like there was too much sea salt in it.

A nod was all she managed, because having the warmth of him that close did all kinds of things to her heart, her mind, her tongue.

He wore a polo shirt she remembered. The one embroidered with the logo of the company he'd told her about quitting right after he decided to sail off into the sunset. The kind of shirt she imagined him wearing with crisp chinos on casual days at the office. Except now, it was weather-beaten and worn: a workingman's shirt with tiny tears, oil stains, and a crumpled collar. Details that said this man was on the run, a little like her. A man going deliciously feral, one tropical day at a time.

He patted her knee and ducked below, and a minute later the engine was on. Julie forced herself to concentrate on what was going on. She'd never been one to follow a man blindly, damn it, and wouldn't start now.

The boat seemed big and small at the same time. Big because all she'd ever been in were little racing hulls, and *Serendipity* was easily three times that size. Thirty-two feet, she remembered Seth saying, plus more for the bowsprit — the spar sticking out from the bow like an older-fashioned whaling ship had. The other boats in the anchorage were patched-up local fishing vessels or fiberglass showpieces that looked like they'd sailed straight out of a glossy magazine. *Serendipity* looked like something out of *Treasure Island*, albeit in miniature. It had dark wood rails and burnished copper-framed portholes. Brass winches and thick wooden pulleys. A spaghetti bowl of lines, running every which way. She could recognize some — the jib sheet, the furling line, the halyard — but had no clue about the others.

"'Scuse me," Tobin said, reaching behind her for a line.

She was in the way. Her shoulder was throbbing, her head spinning.

"Um, mind if I clean up?" she ventured.

Tobin nodded without taking his eyes from Seth, who was busy at the base of the mast. "Make yourself at home."

Three steep steps — ladder rungs, really — and she was in the cabin, feeling a little awed. Just like Seth once told her.

"It's kind of like a camper. A tiny, floating home."

In front of her was a miniature kitchen with a sink, a two-burner stove, and a minuscule countertop squeezed into a corner. Across from it was a table covered by a chart, and on the wall above that was a control panel of switches and electronics: radio, GPS, and other instruments she didn't recognize. All that fit in the tiny space flanking the steps. The rest of the cabin was taken up by a living area created by a U-shaped couch and a built-in table.

It was as cramped as a tiny studio apartment, but cozy too, thanks to the photos and mementos decorating the walls. The space of honor on the far wall was filled by a framed photo of a gray-haired man surrounded by a gaggle of young kids. That had to be the grandfather who'd left Seth and Tobin his boat. She'd bet anything Seth was the serious-looking ten-year-old on the right, holding the tiller. Tobin had to be the mischievous one next to him, tying knots in a line, and the others were sure to be their cousins.

My grandfather died last winter, she remembered Seth saying. He'd left his beloved boat to his grandkids, together with a small sum of money so that each set of siblings might spend some time reconnecting with each other and with the earth.

She let her eyes drift across the happy faces in the photo until they came to rest on the grandfather. Such wise eyes, such a lively face, in spite of all the wrinkles. A man like that, she would have loved to meet.

There were more pictures and postcards hung along the side walls — some old, some new. The most recent ones chronicled the journey the brothers had made from North America: there was a postcard from Charleston, another from Florida, then the Yucatán peninsula, and Belize. Tucked a little deeper along that side of the boat was a recessed bunk with a tousled blanket. Seth's bunk? She leaned in for a closer look and smiled at the titles on the built-in bookshelf, most of them from Patrick O'Brian's *Master and Commander* series. Yep, it was Seth's bunk, all right.

She squinted at the postcard that hung above the pillow. When the lines scribbled on it came into focus, her smile froze and her knees gave way.

Oh my God.

She plopped down onto the mattress, staring at the words.

Chapter Seven

The postcard was hung so the back showed, and the familiar scratchy script was her own.

Gone swimming, she'd written on the postcard, one perfect morning. Julie could remember every detail of it: the whisper of waves over sand, the rise and fall of her sleeping lover's chest. The scent of tropical flowers, filling the morning air.

See you soon! she'd written, then sketched a little scene under the words: two smiling stick figures holding hands.

She clutched her hands together and twisted her fingers around and around. It was the note she'd left for Seth the third or fourth morning of that week they'd spent together. He'd been sleeping like a log, so she'd popped out of the bungalow, gone for a morning swim, then snuck back in for a shower.

Best morning ever, he'd scribbled afterward in a corner of the same card. And that was the truth, because he'd woken up in time to join her in the shower and helped soap her up. Up, down, and sideways, in fact.

A perfect morning, she'd added in the margin. They'd followed the shower with brunch and smoothies on the beach. She could practically hear the sigh of contentment written between the lines.

Perfect sunset, said a later entry. She remembered how the bands of red, gold, and orange melted into each other as Seth's reverent voice told her about his grandfather and the trip south. That night, his gesturing hands and vivid eyes had swept her off her feet for the second time.

She swallowed hard as the lines on the card blurred out of focus.

Seth kept the card.

He kept the memories. Right where he could see them, every morning, every night.

Footsteps sounded on the deck overhead, and she tracked them with her eyes.

Maybe he hadn't run out on her after all. Maybe that Friday had hurt him as much as it hurt her.

She squeezed her eyes shut, fighting the hot, itchy feeling building behind them.

"Ready?" Seth called to Tobin outside.

Snap out of it, already. She was the captain of this misadventure, not a passenger. It was time for action, not regrets. She sucked in a deep breath and climbed back into the cockpit just as Seth came the other way and flicked the corners of his lips up in a fortifying smile. "You good?"

Of course she was good. She was looking into those incredible eyes, and they were smiling back at her.

"Good," she whispered.

He patted her back, and all she could think of was the note over his bunk. Then he ducked below, disappearing into the forward cabin she hadn't explored.

Move. Act. Do something. She looked forward over the cockpit awning, blinking in the midday sun. Tobin was loosening lines bundled at the base of the mast.

"What can I do?" she called out.

Tobin grinned and pointed with an elbow. "See that line?"

"This one? The mainsheet?"

His eyes registered surprise and he grinned wider. "You know boats."

She threw her hands up in protest. "I know small boats."

"Same thing," he said in that breezy manner of his. As if raising the huge sail on a thirty-footer was anything like raising the sail on a tiny dinghy. "Let the mainsheet loose then go back there and unlock the wheel."

She did as told and stood behind the steering wheel, chewing her lip. Her fingers tapped an uncertain rhythm as she eyed the long expanse of deck ahead. The boat looked bigger from here. A lot bigger.

But Tobin was right, as it turned out. The process of getting a big boat underway wasn't all that different from getting a small boat going. It's just that the waterline was farther down, the outlook a little grander.

Soon, the sail was up and Seth was back on deck. He went forward while Tobin came to stand beside Julie at the wheel. He didn't take her place, though. Just stood beside her, watching Seth prepare to weigh anchor.

They were going to let her steer?

She clenched the wheel tighter, listening to her heartbeat pulse in her ears.

Seth glanced back to exchange nods with Tobin then started hauling up the anchor chain. The stories he'd had told her about sailing with his brother had all been accompanied by subtle eye rolls and sighs, but to her eye, they worked like a perfect team.

A sweaty, shirtless team. Every time Seth bent and hauled up another length of thick anchor chain, the muscles in his back corded tight, standing out in all shapes and sizes. Bulky trapezoids bracketed his shoulder blades while parallel lines of muscle wrapped around his sides. Her stomach fluttered at the memory of all the times she'd run her hands over that back and dreamed of running away with him.

Well, she was running now, all right. Just not the way she had imagined.

Seth raised a fist in some kind of signal, and Tobin nodded beside her.

"Anchor's off the bottom. Ease the engine into forward," he coached. "Start turning that way."

She followed his directions, and though the morning had exhausted her, it felt good to focus on the mechanics of the boat.

"That's it, that way." Tobin's voice had just enough of an encouraging lilt to give her a boost of confidence without sounding condescending. When Seth told her his brother was a ski and surf instructor, she figured it meant beach and snow bum. But maybe he was the real thing.

"Perfect," Tobin murmured. "Now straighten it out."

Funny how the world — and people — looked different from the deck of a boat. Seth was making his way back to the cockpit, and he looked different too. With his eyes checking the sail then scanning the anchorage, he looked every inch a captain. Like a man who'd honed his leadership skills in a busy office, then found his true calling on the sea. He wasn't the blustery, pompous kind of captain, but one with a healthy respect for the ocean. The kind you'd trust your life with.

Which, she supposed, was fitting.

When she first met Seth, there was that sense of a butterfly emerging from its cocoon. Clearly, the tropics were freeing him from the cage of family expectations he'd hinted at in conversation. Now, two months later, the change was even more evident. What had been a reddish tint to his skin was all bronze now, the worry lines smoothed. But his eyes were harder, like a man who'd weathered an unexpected storm. A man who'd tasted bitterness and knew how much it hurt to lose something.

Or someone.

Seth turned and looked at her at exactly that moment, his eyes full of unspoken regrets.

Maybe she hadn't been dreaming about how good that week with him had been.

Seth jumped back into the cockpit and adjusted the lines then watched as the mainsail filled with a snap and took shape. He unfurled the smaller forward jib and turned the engine off, letting the breeze carry *Serendipity* away from the mainland. Julie looked back at the palm-lined shore, glad for every inch of watery moat separating her from the men who'd chased her.

"Where to?" Tobin asked.

A quiet minute ticked by before she realized both brothers were looking at her.

She would have shrugged if it weren't for her hurt shoulder. "Anywhere that's away is good with me."

"Over there," Seth pointed. "Behind those islands. Out of sight."

The *out of sight* part sounded as appealing as the low, leafy islands looked. All around them, the sea was a brilliant green-blue lined with occasional ribbons of froth that marked the reefs. The breeze generated by their forward motion was cool, and Julie pulled the beach towel over her shoulders like a cape. Not that she made much of a superhero. Not today.

Seth stood quietly, the wind ruffling his hair as his eyes picked out a route ahead.

Something inside her gave a little nod. This man, she could trust with her life.

"What's behind those islands?" she finally asked.

"Cayo Coco," he said.

She turned her gaze to the horizon.

Cayo Coco. It had a *Treasure Island* kind of ring to it.

Chapter Eight

The sun set not long after they anchored off Cayo Coco. One of those glorious tropical sunsets in which the sky went from perfect blue to bold streaks of yellow, orange, and red in a matter of minutes. The sun winked as it slipped out of view exactly as the full moon rose on the opposite horizon.

Julie held back the sigh building in her throat. The tropical sunset of her dreams, including a boat and a deserted island dotted by palms, all of them whispering in the breeze.

Except there was nothing romantic about this getaway. There was the wound on her shoulder, for one, and a couple of other minor details, like a gang of mysterious bandits who'd chased her for reasons she couldn't explain. And other than the fact that Tobin was there, acting as chaperone, there was also the fact that she still wasn't ready to forgive Seth for leaving her without a word, two months ago. Since then, every day was another day alone, not another day of freedom to do whatever the hell she liked. The independent streak she'd always had was gone with the wind, replaced with a hollowness that work and adventure just couldn't fill. How dare this man do that to her? How dare he?

Somehow, though, she couldn't work up the anger any more.

"Hey," Seth said once the colors deepened. His voice was as soft as the waves sliding over the not-so-distant beach. He could put her to sleep with that voice that promised everything would somehow be all right. "Come inside. Let me have a look at your shoulder."

He had every right to grill her about the motorcycle chase, to ask a dozen questions about the trouble she was in and who and what and why. She could sense the questions building on the tip of his tongue. But he bit them all back, giving her time. The man was a prince.

She followed him inside then plopped down on the couch. A herd of elephants could stampede past her at that moment and she wouldn't react; she was that drained.

Seth peeled back the beach towel and promptly muttered. "Christ."

Julie closed her eyes. Her shoulder wasn't all that bad. It's just that she was tired. Really tired.

His footsteps wandered away, then came back, and something rustled near her ear. Seth was opening a first aid kit and clucking over her shoulder like a mother hen. A little like he had that time they'd gone scuba diving together during that wonderful week. Of course, on that occasion, he'd checked over her air tank and regulator, not a bloody wound. She closed her eyes just as she'd done back then, letting his hands rove, touching down here, then there. His minty breath made its own little breeze in her hair, and the scent of him — sunblock, testosterone, and a deliciously salty tang — gave her a little high.

And God, those hands. Strong and capable yet gentle and warm. She'd had those hands all over her, once upon a time. Those fingers. That murmur in her ear.

She blinked. It wasn't *then*. This was now, and *now* was completely different. His lips on her ear weren't whispering to ask how she liked it, but if she was okay.

"Okay," she echoed, feeling far, far away.

"I need to clean the wound." His hands tugged her sleeve. "Can you take your shirt off, or should I cut it off?"

Her hands flew to her stomach, clutching the fabric against her waist. "It's my favorite shirt."

He eyed it dubiously, and she looked down. Shit. Her favorite T-shirt — *Archaeologists Dig Deeper* — was covered in blood. Her blood.

"Cut it," she mumbled, and he did. When she opened her eyes again, it was on her equally bloodstained bikini. "Damn, my favorite bikini."

"Mine, too," Seth murmured, and his eyes had a faraway look that said he hadn't forgotten a single detail of their time together.

"You can borrow one of mine," Tobin chipped in.

She shot him a weak smile, and even Seth flashed a little grin. Seth's younger brother sure knew how to lighten things up. She'd always figured Tobin was a player — or a playboy — but he came off better now. Maybe the man couldn't help his own charm and good looks.

Then she caught Seth's eyes — those caramel yellow-brown eyes — and she got lost all over again. Swimming in them, wanting to plunge in there and let him make everything okay, wanting his hands on more than just her shoulder. They gazed at each other for an eternity until Tobin cleared his throat, startling Seth back into action.

"It's gonna sting," Seth said, pushing aside the bikini strap and closing in with antiseptic.

It already stings. Being this close to the man who'd left her cold — that stung, big-time. The man she'd fallen for in the space of one night, then fallen deeper for over the days that followed. The man she'd tried to hate over the past couple of months.

The man touching her so carefully, so tenderly, that the couple of tears that slipped out of her eyes weren't from the minor pain of her wound.

He stopped and leaned down until his forehead was resting on hers.

"Jesus, Julie."

That choke behind the whisper? That was for her. Worry that she could have been much more badly hurt.

One of her hands found his and squeezed. "It's not so bad."

"Could have been."

He swallowed, hard, and she couldn't resist threading her fingers the rest of the way through his.

"Too damn close," he finished.

Nothing moved but his chest, rising and falling with every shallow breath. She cupped his face and guided his cheek over to hers. He ran a hand over her good shoulder and the rest of the world fell away — Tobin, puttering around by the chart table; the slight bob and rock of the boat; the distant hiss of waves on the reef. Just the two of them again. God, the man felt good — just the right combination of scruffy and smooth. Smelled good — like the seaside after a storm when everything was fresh and promising. Sounded good — even just the slight rustle of his shirt as he breathed.

Tobin banged the lid on the pot. "So, anyone for dinner?"

Their bodies broke apart, but their eyes remained locked.

"Sure," Seth said, frozen in place.

"Sure," Julie whispered, though she'd already forgotten the question.

"Perfect!" Tobin said somewhere behind the rushing sensation in her ears.

Seth pressed a bandage over the wound and left his hand on her shoulder longer than necessary. The bullet had barely grazed her but it was scary all the same. Because it was a bullet that did that. A bullet aimed at her back.

Tobin leaned in to inspect his brother's work. "Lotta blood for something that shallow," he sniffed. "So what were those guys after?" he asked, going back to the spaghetti pot.

Seth stiffened, and she could feel his eyes on her. She kept her gaze down, studiously avoiding the direction of her backpack. "I don't know," she mumbled.

Even as a whisper, it sounded like a lie.

Chapter Nine

Seth watched Julie stand stiffly and pick up her bag. Now that his doctoring was over, he could feel the blood drain from his face, his hand start to shake. For all the nights he'd lain awake, wishing for Julie back, Julie with a bullet wound was not what he had in mind.

Didn't matter, though. She was back now, and this time, he wouldn't let anything get between them. Not chance, not the weather, not lucky or unlucky breaks. Not even gun-toting gangsters.

"Is there someplace I can change?" she murmured, and this time, her eyes avoided his.

His gaze stuck on her bloodstained bikini for a second before he led her to the front cabin. The corridor was narrow, and he and Julie danced around each other for a moment. He could feel her body yearning for the contact as much as his did, because the need to tango, to samba, to get together and churn and grind always seemed to rear up out of nowhere when she got close. But as much as his body wanted it, his mind threw out a hundred warning signs. *Not yet. Caution. Slow down.*

The only part about any of those he liked was the *yet*.

Julie brushed clear of him, into the front cabin. He closed the door behind her then sat down at the chart table. Stared at the instruments, as if that would help him get a grip. That and the postcard of New York a friend had given him in case he missed home. He blinked at it. No, he hadn't missed his job or his home over the past couple of months. Hadn't missed the luxuries of life on land.

The only thing he'd missed at all was her. Julie. The spark of her eyes, the lilt of her voice as she talked. Even better, the way she leaned in to listen as if she wanted to excavate the real him, hidden beneath all the layers piled over the outside.

Something moved at his elbow, and he looked up to find Tobin handing him a glass of wine.

"Want rum instead?" Tobin whispered, the usual humor gone from his voice.

Seth shook his head, tried sipping, not gulping, the wine, and pretended to study the chart while his mind replayed the events of a crazy day.

Julie back in his life. That was good. Great. Serendipitous, even.

Julie in some kind of trouble. Not good.

He glanced at the photograph of his grandfather. "You ever wonder..." he started then trailed off.

"I wonder constantly." Tobin winked then wiped his eyes with his sleeve and went back to chopping onions.

"I mean..." Seth struggled to find the right words. It wasn't often he and his brother had a heart-to-heart. Which showed how right their grandfather was to push them into this trip. It had been good for both of them in a dozen different ways. "You ever wonder about serendipity? Luck? All that?"

Tobin gave the door to the front cabin a pointed look and chuckled out loud. "Man, I only wonder that it's taken you this long to figure it out." He shook his head. "And you're supposed to be the smart one."

"You're just as smart."

"I know, I know. Just a little underachieving." Tobin said it with a smile that smacked of sheer pride. Like it was an accomplishment to achieve as little as he had in life: getting kicked out of two good schools, never settling down to a real job. But then again, coming from their family, maybe that was an achievement. Mom a lawyer, Dad a doctor, paving the way for their sons to do the same. A family name that ensured them good schools, good connections. Seth had followed right along with it, and until this trip, he'd never questioned any of it. But sailing was giving him a different perspective. That there was more to life than insane work hours and the four walls of an office. More than frantic weekdays and all-too-short weekends. More than profits and accounts.

There were sunsets. Chance encounters. The kind of tiredness that comes from time in the sun and fresh air. New faces and the stories that came with each of them.

"Maybe you're the smart one," Seth said, looking at his brother. Maybe Tobin hadn't been wasting his life, the way their mother always complained that he did. Tobin never stressed, never rushed to meetings, never failed to enjoy life.

His younger brother's eyes sparkled at his comment. "Wish I had a tape recorder for that one." Then he grew more serious. "Do things happen for a reason? I don't know. But I do know that when they do, you can't just go along for the ride. Remember what he used to say?" He pointed the knife toward the photo on the opposite wall.

Seth could hear their grandfather's gritty voice as if he were sitting across the cabin. *Dream, then go out and do something about it.*

Tobin waggled his eyebrows toward the front cabin. "Just sayin'." Then he went back to work, grabbing a handful of spaghetti and tossing it into the pot.

Dreams. Chance encounters. Serendipity. Seth stared off into the universe in the bottom of his wine glass.

Go out and do something about it.

His gaze wandered to the door separating him from Julie, and he worked his jaw from side to side. Here he was, taking advice from his dead grandfather and his little brother, the ski bum. How messed up was that?

"You're the expert in wild flings with women you barely know," he whispered to Tobin. "Why the hell can't I get over it?"

Tobin laughed. "Doesn't count as a fling if you fall in love, man."

Part of him reeled at the thought; the other part sighed in a pathetic, dreamy way. Which probably meant it was love, because what else in life gave a man that mixture of terror and thrill?

He poured himself another swig.

Julie took a good long while, so long that he started to wonder if she needed help. He was halfway to the separating door when it popped open and she stepped out in a clean bikini — the yellow and blue one — and a different pair of khaki shorts. God, she was something. Sports jock mixed with beauty queen mixed with nerdy academic. What other woman combined all three?

"Just in time!" Tobin called. "Who's for dinner?"

Seth looked Julie up and down, and just like that, his appetite was back.

"Me," Julie said, looking right into his eyes.

"Me," he whispered, looking right back.

Chapter Ten

Apparently, Julie had an appetite, too. Seth watched her chow right through Tobin's spiced-up version of spaghetti bolognese, then went through seconds and wiped the bowl clean with a piece of bread. She laughed right through Tobin's stories and marveled as the stars arched overhead on a perfectly peaceful night. But she didn't meet Seth's eyes, not for longer than a second, nor did she move any closer into the narrow strip of space he'd been careful to leave when they sat next to each other. All in all, she was doing a great job avoiding the unavoidable, just as Tobin was doing a great job sticking to harmless topics and offbeat jokes.

No questions about what the hell was going on, no demands. She wasn't ready for it; both of them could sense it. Even though his brother had every right to ask, he didn't. Tobin kept the tone light and easy, building up her trust, her confidence.

And here Seth had spent the past thirty-one years of his life thinking his little brother was complete dead weight. Go figure.

"Two surfers are at getting ready to paddle out to a break. Know what they say?" Tobin winked at Julie.

"What?"

"The first guy says, 'Guess what? I got a new longboard for my wife¡"

"And the second guy says. . . ?" she prompted him.

" 'Great trade!' "

As usual, Tobin folded into chuckles at his own joke, but even Seth had to smile when Julie did. Exhaled, actually, when he saw that she didn't hang too closely on his brother's every word. No fluttering of eyelashes, no loud giggles. The charm machine that was his brother wasn't making any headway tonight, just like Tobin hadn't made any headway the very first time they'd met. It was Seth she fell for. Just like he'd fallen for her.

Hard. Fast. Deep.

Seth blinked at Tobin. The guy who normally went after every girl — any girl — was keeping a careful distance. Entertaining, not seducing, for once in his life. Tobin even had the tact to take the dishes at the end of dinner and disappear into the galley, leaving Seth and Julie alone.

Still, thirty-two feet of boat was a little too little space for all that he and Julie had to discuss.

"Hey," Seth ventured, nudging her thigh. The first contact they'd made all night, and it made his skin tingle. His heart, too, because she didn't pull away. "How about we head to shore?"

She looked at the little spit of land, her face showing both temptation and fright. He felt exactly the same way: desperate for time alone with her, terrified where their conversation might lead.

He nudged her again, pulling out his ace. "Come on, it'll be an adventure." Then he caught himself and added, "A small, safe one."

She laughed, and her hand slid across his arm just like he remembered it doing their first time around. "Okay."

And they were off in the dinghy, slaloming through the shadows that marked coral heads. He cut the engine ten yards off the beach and let the little inflatable coast in.

"Land ho," he said, very quietly. It was a tiny island, but it felt like a major landfall after all they'd experienced that crazy day.

He stepped into ankle-deep water and Julie followed suit. A born sailor; his grandfather would have approved.

Together, they hauled the dinghy up on shore and considered the little spit of land. One hundred yards of sand, palm, and coconuts wasn't much space, but in the moonlight, it seemed to go on forever.

"Oooh!" Julie pointed up. "A shooting star!"

Make a wish, he could practically hear her think. He knew exactly what he wished for, so he did. Sent that wish right up to the stars without even pausing to think what kind of sap this sailing gig was turning him into. Wishing on stars? Getting hung up on a woman? Appreciating his little brother? He wasn't just thousands of miles from home — he was a different man.

"Julie, we need to talk," he said, even as she strode away from the dinghy. "Wait. . ."

Tiny bits of coral crunched underfoot as he followed her. Palm fronds swished overhead, hanging at steep angles. Julie took three more steps then stopped. Her hair fell back as she tipped her chin up, and the set of her shoulders told him she'd rather not talk about any of it. Not about today, not about the past.

He expected a comment about black holes or nebulae or the craters of the moon, but she was quiet. And then he realized why. Why her face was glistening, her eyes squeezed shut. He saw her swipe at the tears, heard her mutter a curse at herself.

"Julie?"

He wanted to wrap his arms around her and tell her that even tough-as-nails archaeology jocks were allowed to cry. Kiss her ear and promise her that somehow, he'd make everything all right.

"You okay?"

She flapped a hand at the horizon as if she wanted to divert his attention there. "It's so beautiful." And it was: the endless ocean, the indigo sky.

"So why are you crying?"

Her hand did the jitterbug and her voice shook. "I'm all mixed up."

No kidding. He was, too. The chase. The gun aimed at her back earlier in the day. Sitting through dinner with a thousand questions and no answers. Being this close to her again.

The next thing he knew, he'd closed the distance and folded her in his arms. Pulled her back into his chest and felt her take a long, deep breath then settle against him with a sigh.

God, it felt good to hold a woman who didn't need much holding. To smell Julie's special scent again, a blend of rain forest-fresh skin and coconut-shampoo hair. To feel her heat. To wipe away the tears and put his cheek against hers.

Absolutely perfect. Even the tears, because he knew Julie wasn't one to open up often. And she was doing it for him.

Trusting. Relaxing. With him.

She sniffed a little and wrapped her arms over his, making the hug tighter. Even when she shook her head and muttered at herself, she stayed close.

"What?" he whispered.

"Seth, I barely even know you."

He turned her slowly so he could look her in the eyes. "You know me better than anyone I've ever known."

It was true. Sometimes he thought she knew him better than he knew himself. Because for years, he hadn't been living so much as filling a role. The responsible older brother. The good son. The business jock. Fresh air and salt water had slowly scoured those superficial layers off, and even he was surprised what was showing underneath. A guy who could spend an hour watching the clouds move overhead. Who could look at the horizon and not need to know exactly where he'd go next.

A guy who could fall in love in the space of one week. Not just with anyone. With her.

She lowered her head to his chest but didn't let go of him. "I don't even know where you're from."

"Boston," he shot right out, ready to do anything to convince her. "Lexington. Next?" He waved an impatient hand. What was it going to take to convince her he was serious? "Ask me. Ask me anything."

Her face lifted and said, *That's not the point.*

He stepped back and set his feet wide like he was about to push a big boulder up a very steep hill. "I like coffee black and tea white. I like soccer over football. Thrillers over nonfiction. I hate skim milk."

She stared, so he went on.

"I grew up with my brother and a basset hound named Cleo. We always went sailing with my grandfather in the summers — us and our cousins. On *Serendipity*—" he pointed across the water "—which is why he left it to us. Me, Tobin, and our other cousins. And you know what? He was totally right. We were getting out of touch with each other. And with everything else." He waved a hand at the night sky, the inky horizon, the ocean. Back home he never even knew what phase the moon was in; out here, he could feel the pull of the tide, smell the slightest shift in the wind.

"We were supposed to have a little sister, but she was stillborn." It hurt a little to say it out loud, but it felt good, too. His family never talked about it, and that was wrong. It had taken him years to understand why his parents came home from the hospital looking so hollow, why they'd clutched him that tightly. Why he and Tobin had each reacted the way they had: Seth becoming the dutiful older son, trying to make things better for parents who would never be consoled, while Tobin became a rebel without a cause, insisting on living large and loud just to spite death.

On the other hand, maybe it hadn't taken him years to figure that out. The sea had unwrapped those mysteries for him within the space of a couple of weeks. Funny how time and space could clean out the mess of a man's head.

"Her name was Linda. And no, my parents never got over it."

Julie's jaw dropped.

He went straight on before his throat closed up on the choke building in the back. "In eleventh grade I got caught smoking behind the gym and was suspended for a week. My closest brush with the law — until now." He tried a little smile. "The first woman I ever slept with was my best friend's older sister, the summer she was back from college. Brenda. She had a snake tattoo around her belly button no one was supposed to know about."

Julie's eyebrow shot up.

He was building momentum now, so why not roll on with this out-of-control train? "I've never been outside the US or

Mexico. Never done it in the back seat of a car. Never had the guts to break out of the mold until I did this trip. And I never met anyone like you."

He gulped. Silence closed in as the sea breeze fluttered his hair. His fingers plucked at the hem of his shorts. Damn, where had all that come from? He closed his eyes and wondered how soon Julie would demand that he take her back to the boat, back to solid land, and kick him out of her life once and for all.

But there was nothing but the sound of his own near-panting breath and the swish of the waves on the beach. Then a gentle hand on his cheek and a soft, moist touch on his lips, and Julie was in his arms, hugging him tight. He clamped his arms around her and went limp with relief.

The kiss got wider, deeper, hungrier, and then she pulled back, her hands fisted in his shirt. "Some speech, sailor."

He put his hands over hers and smoothed them flat against his chest, relishing the connection. "I never wanted to hurt you. Never wanted to leave you."

She leaned her forehead on his shoulder and stroked his back in silence.

"So what happened?" she whispered at last. "That Friday?"

Chapter Eleven

What happened? Seth ground his teeth together. They'd nearly lost the boat because of Tobin's mistake. Even now, he could flay his brother's hide. Then again, as captain, he was just as much to blame for not being more tuned in.

"The weather," he started.

Julie snapped back and slapped his arm, her face taking on an angry hue he could see even in the moonlight. "Don't give me some story about the weather. It was perfect. Blue sky, no wind."

He put his hands up. "No, not that!" His voice was too loud, too sharp, though, so he started again. "Listen, it's true. There's a thing called a north swell."

She stuck her hands on her hips and drew her lips into a thin line, but at least she hadn't turned her back and stomped away. Yet.

"North swell," she said with a scary lack of intonation in her voice.

"Yes, a north swell. Look, the ocean is always moving, right?"

She made a face that said he had ten seconds to get to the point.

"Wind pushes the sea into waves, and big storms make big waves. So big that even when the storm dies out, the waves roll on." His hand undulated in the air to demonstrate, which was good, because her focus went there and away from his chin, which she looked about to clobber. He swung his left hand toward his right in little scooping motions, like the wind stoking the waves. "And if you keep some wind direction acting on those waves — that swell can travel thousands of miles and eventually come up in a totally different place."

"Like here? Santa Marta?" she asked dubiously.

"Like Santa Marta." He nodded. "I was coming to meet you, just like I said I would — Jesus, I wouldn't have missed it! — but that's when we noticed the boats leaving the harbor. Not one or two boats, but all of them. Even the local fishing boats were hauling ass. Jim from *Dreamtime* motored past us on his way out, saying 'When are you getting the hell out?' We had no idea what was going on until then." Seth dared to reach out to her shoulder then — the uninjured one. "I was supposed to be watching the weather, but I was..." He groped for the right word, because *distracted* would never fly. "Busy with you," he finished. "Not thinking about anything else."

He paused, because shit, did that sound like he was only thinking of sex? He rushed on, willing her to understand. "Stupidly, I let it slide. Tobin said he'd check the weather, but he didn't. And all of a sudden we had eight hours' notice to get to the next spot with decent shelter from the waves coming in from the north."

She cocked her head at him, and he pointed west. "Cayo Largo, over there." Funny how a couple of months of sailing could give a guy an internal compass. "Which was seven hours away and filling up fast with boats." His heart beat faster, just remembering the race to get to shelter in time. To save his grandfather's boat before it could be dashed against the shore by that killer swell.

"So what happened?" She looked anxious, like she'd lived the moment with him. In a way, he wished that she could have, because it would have helped to have her around. Someone with a good head on her shoulders — unlike his brother. Someone whose presence always managed to calm him, the way her touch always did.

He exhaled, both in reliving the moment and from the rush of his words. "We got in after everyone else and barely got the anchor down before it went from a not-so-bad eight-foot swell to a crazy fifteen-feet — and counting. We were way at the back of the pack in deep water. Stood anchor watch, the both of us, for twenty-four hours, with the engine running in case things went bad." His eyelid twitched just at the memory. "Outside the anchorage, the swell built to twenty-five feet in a couple of hours, and it worked its way in. In the end, we did okay. A couple of the other boats dragged and went aground. The rest of us pitched in to help them, but that took two days." Two long days in which all he'd wanted to do was get the hell back to Julie before she left. And then it got worse.

"But even when the swell went down, a storm hit. That was Tuesday. We upped anchor and got to another anchorage with better wind shelter and sat out fifty-knot winds there. Three days of that crap." He wrung his hands in the air. "Believe me, if I could have gotten back, I would have. But first the storm, then the sea was still a mess, then—"

"Seth." She squeezed his arm.

He froze. This was where she'd slap him and say goodbye.

"Seth."

He squeezed his eyes closed, because he deserved whatever she had to scream at him.

"I get it, Seth. I believe you."

"You do?"

Her lips pulled into a tight smile. "I do."

All the air pooled in his lungs fled in a huge rush.

"Really?"

She nodded. "Really."

He pulled her in for a hug and took a couple of deep breaths before going on. "We got back a week later, but. . ."

"But I was gone." Her voice cracked on the last syllable.

He nodded, lost in memories. He'd made a hundred rounds of the town, looking for her, asking after her, wondering how to get in touch.

"You were gone, and I had no way to contact you — no email, no phone, nothing. I tried. I looked up every damn archaeological dig I could, trying to find one starting with Xtla. . . Xtle. . . Xt. . ."

"Xtlemacán," she filled in, the awkward Mayan syllables flowing off her tongue.

"But I couldn't find it. Couldn't find you. I didn't even know your last name." He tightened his hug to hide the shudder going through his body. "We tried everything for two weeks, and then..." He trailed off just short of saying, *I gave up*, even though it was true.

She was swaying gently in his arms now, and all he wanted was to stand there and hold her all night. All week. Hell, a month would be good. The citrus-salt scent of her hair, the light curves of her body pressed into his — yeah, that was good. Better than good.

"So where did you go?" she murmured at last.

He told her the rest, quickly, because it didn't matter any more, not now.

"Tobin promised to meet his friends in Mexico, so we sailed all the way up the coast, then all the way back here. "We're heading south now, to Panama for hurricane season." He couldn't resist a stop in Santa Marta to try to find her one more time, even though he knew she'd be long gone by then. And even though Tobin complained the whole way about him mooning over some chick.

He'd just about punched his brother. Julie was not just *some chick*.

So what is she? Tobin had asked.

Damned if Seth didn't get stuck on the answer. He stood there, shaking his head, gesturing vaguely in the air. What was Julie to him, exactly?

A hell of a lot more than some chick, was the best he could eventually sputter. Then he'd pulled seniority and insisted they stop in the beach town. And there she'd been, at the Coco Loco Café. Bronzed and beautiful as ever.

And now she was here, on this tiny spit of an island, those sky-blue eyes studying his.

"The whole time, all I wanted was you." He hesitated on the cusp of his confession then let the dam break. What did he have to lose now? "Julie, I still want you. And not just for a week. Not for a month. I want..." He caught himself there, sounding like the self-centered bastard he probably was. *I want, I want, I want.*

"What do you want?" she prompted, so softly he barely caught the words.

"I want a chance. With you. To give us a try."

There. He'd said it. Even if she shot him down with every weapon in her arsenal until he was limp and bleeding in a pathetic heap, at least he'd have tried. He didn't want a fling. He wanted a shot at more. Maybe even forever.

If he hadn't already blown it, that is.

She was awfully quiet for a minute. Watching him, looking more tired and lost than she'd looked all day. She opened her mouth, and he wanted to coax the words out. Words like *I want that, too, Seth. I want to give us a try.*

Her shoulders drooped and her chin dropped to her chest. "I can't think straight, Seth. I have people chasing me. Men with guns—"

"I'll help you," he blurted.

"You already have."

He shook his head. "No, right through to the end. 'Til we figure this out. Do whatever it takes to get them off your back, or to get you out of Belize. Whatever it takes."

She glanced up, eyes shiny with...hope? Tears? He couldn't tell which.

"We?"

"We." He hammered the word out to make sure she believed, then sealed his lips, because if he said one more word, he'd probably screw everything up.

He gulped and listened to his heart kick madly inside his chest, waiting...until she slid into his arms and pulled herself close. He knotted his hands behind her and let his eyes shut in a silent promise. Somehow, he'd get her out of her mess. Somehow, he'd keep her safe.

And after that, he'd make sure he never screwed up with her again.

Chapter Twelve

On a scale of ten, that hug was at least a twelve, Julie decided. The bonus points were for those thick arms, circling her just tightly enough to squeeze her body against his without impeding the rise and fall of her lungs. The steady beat of his heart was like a metronome for hers to follow, instead of galloping in panic at all that had gone wrong.

She'd never needed Seth to comfort her before, but he was good at that, too. She didn't want to need comfort as much as this, but... it felt good. The weight of his head against hers, showing that he wasn't staring over her shoulder or checking his watch but snuggled good and close like the two of them were a couple of sleepy sheep.

Except the longer the hug lasted, the less sleepy she felt. Quite the opposite, in fact, since their combined heat seemed to be pooling low in her core. Her hips nudged closer and closer to his while her leg kept wanting to play python and glide around his.

It took the last of her willpower to pull away — everything but her left hand, which refused to let his go. She tilted her head to one side, and they walked wordlessly along the beach.

It felt like their very first night together, yet nothing like it at all. This strange mix of cozy and awkward and excited was the same. In Santa Marta, though, everything had been fun and games. It all seemed so simple at the time: the sand, the sun, the bungalow with its queen-sized bed, beckoning them inside. His body and hers, fitting together perfectly. No false promises, no heavy emotions. Just a week of fun.

At least, that's what she'd told herself. Even as the days and nights of that magical week cycled toward the inevitable goodbye, she went on lying, or at least procrastinating. Because they were supposed to have had that final fun Friday together, then a Saturday to deal with goodbye.

But then that Friday had rolled around, and everything fell apart. She'd gone straight back to work and straight back to lying to herself — that Seth didn't matter to her. That he hadn't kindled an inner fire that refused to go out.

The fire burning brightly under this perfect tropical night. She tightened her fingers around his, and the inner flames blazed higher still.

"Nice island," she whispered just to fill the silence.

The palms all seemed to lean in to eavesdrop, and a seagull dipped closer, the white of its wings flashing in the moonlight.

"Hmmm," Seth agreed, pulling her hand up and holding it against his abdomen. "Nice place."

It was all she could do not to run her fingers over the ridges of muscle under his skin. Because yeah, the place was nice, but not at all conducive to keeping a clear head or thinking about more important things, like the mysterious gangster-cops chasing her earlier in the day.

No, this idyllic splotch of sand in a turquoise sea was just not the place for thoughts like that. More like the place to lean left so her side was pressed along his. The place to let her arm slide around his back while they walked and let him do the same.

This island was perfect for all that. So perfect that they eventually stopped walking and folded in on each other, coming face-to-face. She turned into Seth's chest, and her eyes didn't have time to check his because she pressed right into a kiss.

A long, soft kiss that was like the sea: it seemed to go on forever, and she didn't want it to end. The kind of kiss that wouldn't stay innocent for long. Not with the waves whispering, the palms giggling, the stars smiling overhead.

It was just like their second or third kiss of their very first night together — the one that followed the first couple of shy touches, right before that wave of desire knocked both of them over and swept them away.

Just like that. She let her tongue trace the whole perimeter of his lips, then delve deeper to tease his into action. She flattened her breasts against his chest, squeezing every ion of air out from between them, rubbing against him like a lioness with her mate. Which wasn't far off, considering the purring kind of rumble building in his chest. Though lions, of course, didn't slide their paws into the waistline of each other's shorts.

He brought his lips to her ear and focused his kisses there a while before pulling in a long, heavy breath. "Julie."

She shook her head and brought his lips back to hers. What was there to discuss? Everything was a consuming light, pulling her toward him. She needed contact, not words. She needed him.

"Julie."

She kissed right through it like they were back to that Friday and nothing would keep them apart.

"Julie..."

She slumped in his arms. What was the difference between this night and all their other times together when he hadn't shown the slightest hesitation?

The moon shone the answer right back at her. That was then, this was now. And this time, there was more at stake. This wasn't sex any more. It was more.

"Don't you dare go all gentlemanly on me," she mumbled into his shirt. "Because I prefer the pirate."

His perfect lips curled up at the ends. "I don't want to stop, but this pirate's pockets are empty."

It took her hazy mind a minute to figure that out. No condom. The slutty part of her mind sent her hands tunneling into his pockets, conducting a thorough search. No condom, but there was a handful of something else. More than a handful, in fact. She ran her fingertips against the length of his cock and smiled at the quiver that produced.

"Pity," she murmured. It was sort of a compliment, in a way. Maybe he didn't just want to use her for sex. Maybe not all men had one-track minds.

Then she let a secret smile spread across her face as she pulled his hands toward her pockets and guided them in. A rustle ensued and Seth cracked a huge grin.

"You don't."

"I do." She smiled into his lips, feeling ridiculously pleased with herself. Never mind what it suggested about women and their one-track minds. In truth, she'd been cleaning up in the tiny bathroom on *Serendipity* when the condoms fell out of her bag, and she'd pocketed them without thinking. But maybe her subconscious had been at work, because something about Seth did that to her. That combination of *really nice guy* and *buccaneer*.

"Here I am being all gentlemanly while you're being a vixen," he murmured.

"I prefer pirate, thank you very much." She rolled her sandal over the rough coral underfoot. "Though, I have to admit, I've never had my way with a man on an uninhabited island. How about you?"

"Had my way with a man?"

She play-slapped him then ran the hand down his hip. A tiny tremor went through him, making her pulse spike.

"Have you ever rescued a helpless damsel in distress and kissed her on a deserted tropical island?" She held her breath, suddenly not sure she wanted to know. Maybe he'd been charming women all the way down the coast. He and that brother of his...

He snorted and shifted so their bodies were perfectly aligned. "You're no helpless damsel."

"I was today."

"You scaled a ten-foot wall with glass on top!"

"Eight feet. Nine, tops."

"You jumped on the back of a speeding motorcycle."

She had to laugh at that one. "You were barely moving."

"I was going at least thirty."

She shook her head, then caught him in a kiss that sent another flaring zing through her body. "Sailor's choice: palm tree, or missionary style on the beach?"

His head went up to the crown of the nearest palm. "Tree?"

"I mean against it, not up it."

His eyes lit up enough to show her he'd probably had that fantasy, too, but never actually tried it. A hand slid against her shorts and the package rustled again.

"How many condoms you have in there?"

Heat rushed to her face because, yeah, that felt good. To be wanted — and more than once — ahead of time.

"Two."

He nodded, and the impish look was gone, replaced by something dark and hungry. "Then I vote for the tree." He was already backing her toward the nearest trunk, all pirate now, dark and gritty and hungry. "Then we'll find a smooth patch of sand where I can lay you down and watch your face in the moonlight when I touch you."

His words were like a third hand, gliding down her spine. Because the pirate was a poet — a poet who could make her panties wet without a single touch. Because the subtext was there: *I want to watch your face in the moonlight when I screw you senseless. I want to make it good for you and for me.*

Those promises, she couldn't wait for him to make good on. She was already clutching at his shirt, wishing it were gone.

"Touch me where?" she asked, all husky now. Because her back was against the trunk of the palm and his hips were squeezing against hers. Hard.

"Nuh-uh." He shook his head. "Not giving the whole pirate fantasy away too soon." He traced the lower edge of her bikini top and she pressed more tightly against him.

"Doesn't have to be a fantasy, sailor."

Chapter Thirteen

"Good," Seth whispered, though he might as well have yelled *Go!* because the two of them were off and away. His mouth got busy with her neck, nipping between kisses and she couldn't help but let her head loll back against the tree. He slid his hands across her back and tugged at the bikini strap that stuck out from the collar of her shirt. Then both shirt and bikini were shucked and dangling from her hands — because it was she who'd tugged them both off. It was her hurrying him on, because this was a hell of a lot better than fear and uncertainty and where-the-hell-do-I-go-next. This was warm and accepting and safe, because behind that pirate was a prince of a man who'd give her every pleasure, satisfy every urge.

Seth's broad hands cupped her breasts and lifted as his thumbs teased her nipples into straining peaks. She closed her eyes and let all her senses feast on his touch. His sailor's hands were like massage pads, switching from coarse scrub to soft rub as different parts of his palms and fingers touched her. Her shoulders were flexing backward, all but wrapping themselves around the tree — anything to give him more access. Breath became a form of speech as she huffed and sighed her pleasure into the night.

"You like that," he chuckled.

She gulped and nodded. The man could tie her upside down from this tree and she'd like it. He'd always managed that trick — finding her inner switch and flipping it. Gone with the capable, independent woman, in with the whimpering beast.

He grinned and followed the curve of her body down like a slide, peppering kisses as he went. She wanted to howl for more because he was waking every primal urge in her soul. She laced her hands through his hair and eased him away from the plump side of one breast to the nipple, but damned if the man didn't skim right over it on the first pass. But just when she was about to protest, he darted back, latched on, and sucked.

"Oh God," she mumbled, letting her head thunk back against the tree. Seth could make her high just from his touch. The stars were already looking like blurry swirls of light. A whole art gallery of constellations stretched overhead, winking and cheering her on.

It felt good. It felt…free. Which really didn't make sense — giving herself over to a man completely, even confidently. But nothing about this crazy day made sense. Nothing about the way her body yearned for his from the moment they'd met, all those weeks ago.

Didn't make sense, but instinct said it was right.

Her fingers plucked at his shirt, working desperately to get it off. He must have chuckled out of the side of his mouth, because she could feel the bounce of his lips on her breast along with the sound. He leaned back in a squat, yanked his shirt off — zoom, a whole checkerboard of muscle bared to her eyes — and then he was back, sucking her nipple into his mouth then letting it out slowly. In, then out, until the sound of the ocean in her ears was a roar.

This was just what she remembered — and what she'd tried to forget — of their carefree week together. Seth had always given her everything before asking for anything in return. His only hurry was achieving her pleasure, and he worked her higher and higher until her body thrummed with desperate need.

He leaned right to play with the other breast then slid down to her navel. For one breathtaking minute she thought he might go lower still. Her hands might just have nudged his head in that direction, except he straightened instead and took her mouth in a plundering kiss. The whole weight of him was against her now, the smooth plates of his chest squeezing against her breasts, his sculpted shoulders under her hands. All he needed was a beard and he'd be Neptune, come out of the sea to take his pleasure with the woman of his choice.

Her. Plain old her. She was his top choice. Her whole body quivered.

The breeze kicked up a notch and she worked her hands down his body, pushing his shorts down until he kicked them off, then let her explore. She let her hands scoop behind to admire the powerful slab of his ass before slipping around the front to fist his cock. He sucked in a deep breath, and she did, too, because the man really was a god, too big to be true. But the building moisture between her legs promised it would be an easy ride. A good ride. Hell, a magical ride.

She slid her hand toward the bulging head of his cock then rode back up, tugging the foreskin as she went.

His head went heavy on her shoulder, but the bulk of him went stiff as he groaned. "Ju..."

Good to know she wasn't the only one losing it here.

"You like that," she murmured.

"Like?" He shook his head slightly, whispering, "Like is not the word."

She repeated the heady ride, imagining him sliding inside her body instead of in her hand. Her legs twitched with anticipation, her breasts swelling full and hard. She slid down the full length of him, let a finger circle his crown, then dragged up until her fist was nested in the curls at the base. She paused there, feeling him pulse in her hand.

"Do it again." His voice was hoarse, like he'd been screaming his pleasure inside.

She did it again and again until he shuddered and went perfectly still, fighting the urge to come. She was tempted to keep working him with her hand, just to watch this chunk of a man unravel at her touch.

"Wait." With his chin on her shoulder, she could feel him gulp. "Wait."

She stood perfectly still, caged between his body and the tree. Loving it there. Loving the weight of him in her hand.

He let out a long, deep breath as if he was in control again, but the look in his eye when he glanced at her said he was close, very close.

Something fumbled at her side: his hand, dipping into her pocket.

"I'll be needing this now," he said, shaking his head as if he couldn't quite believe what he was doing. The man liked being in control of himself just as much as she liked pushing him over the edge.

"Then I won't be needing these," she teased and slid her shorts slowly down her hips.

His eyes followed every inch even as his fingers unrolled the condom over his length.

She thought that would be the moment — he'd step closer, lift her, enter her. Bring her the release her body craved. But apparently, the man had one more trick in mind.

He drew her arms up over her head and pinned them against the tree, leaning so close, she could feel the insistent jut of his erection against her belly. His eyes were locked on hers, watching her reaction as he dragged his body against hers, lifting up an inch, then pulling down, like he still had to undress her but didn't want to use his hands. Letting his cock ride up and down her belly until all she wanted was him in, in, in.

With her hands trapped, her options were limited. She curled a leg behind his calf and slid it high. Higher. She canted her leg sideways, opening her core to him. He dipped and pressed hard into her groin.

"Seth," she whispered. She wanted to grab his ass and guide him home, but the man just wouldn't give in. Every ripple of his body, every slow thrust of his cock was winding her up like one of those rubber band helicopters she used to play with as a kid — tighter and tighter until she thought she would snap. But he kept putting in another turn, and another, telling her he wasn't quite ready to release his creation and let her fly, fly, fly.

"You know you want in," she murmured. Her voice had gone all thick and sultry, but hell, this was too good to hold back for.

His nostrils flared, and she hauled him closer, thrusting her hips forward to let him feel her heat.

"I do want in." He nodded. "Deep in."

"So take me, pirate," she whispered, wiggling her fingers against his.

His eyes were dark pools around tiny points of light, focused entirely on her. But he was waiting. Waiting for... Waiting for what? She was ready, she was begging, she was fighting for more—

Her breath hitched. Fighting. That was it. Every sinew in her body was tight and straining, every muscle clenched. He'd commented on that once.

You always this wound up? he'd asked.

You make me this wound up, she countered.

He'd stroked her hair gently. *Relax.*

Sex had never seemed like a time to relax, not to her, so she'd arched an eyebrow in challenge.

Don't relax everything, he chuckled. *Just the parts that count.* He leaned closer. *Trust me.*

Didn't he know how long it had been since she'd truly trusted someone? Let herself relax?

He was saying the same thing now. *Relax. Trust.*

But this time, that trust wasn't just about her body. It was about her heart. Was she willing to give any man that?

She closed her eyes and focused on the pattern of his breath, the rise and fall of his chest. She drew the scent of him deep into her lungs and let the muscles of her legs, her arms, and her back unwind. Let her fingers go limp in his, one at a time. Took another deep breath and told herself to let go.

Then she opened her eyes on him and let them say the words that couldn't quite cross her lips. *I trust you.*

His eyes glimmered and he smiled like a satisfied feline. Slowly, surely, he lowered her hands to his shoulders, tipped one shoulder down, and hitched her leg higher on his waist. Then he lifted the other one, picking her up off the ground like she weighed nothing and held her high, poised over the crown of his cock.

Trust. Relax.

When he spoke, his voice was gritty as thick sand. "Ready, m'lady?"

Was she ever. "Ready, pirate."

"Good," he added, his voice dropping low. "Because I want in. Deep in."

Chapter Fourteen

Seth forced himself to catalog all the sensations throwing themselves at him. The fresh jungle scent that followed Julie everywhere she went; the growl of her voice against the smooth roll of waves on the beach. The feel of the lumpy coral underfoot. The pale light of the moon, showing her need. The tree behind Julie was hard, but the flesh of her breasts was soft. The rest of her was taut and toned and straining for him.

Welcoming him. Trusting him, even.

That part went to his head like a drug, because even in the week they'd spent together, she'd never ventured that far. The woman was like a treasure chest — always with a new secret, a new gem. And only open to him. The way she hesitated told him she'd never opened this far to any man. Virgin territory, in its own way.

Which made for the best kind of anticipation — even better than the first time with her that night on the beach on Santa Marta. Because he didn't have to wonder how good it would be. He knew exactly how tight she'd be around him. How wet. How lost in the burning instinct to mate.

It was a miracle he'd made it this far with as much control, because every one of Julie's touches lit another blaze until he was on completely on fire.

"Seth," she moaned, drawing his name out as he lowered her slowly onto his cock.

The gradual dip, the sensation of slipping along her heated inner walls had him burning for more, fighting an inner urge to plunge straight home. But slow was good. Slow was perfect.

Slow was heaven.

He pushed his hips forward until he had her hard against the tree. Her eyes slid closed.

"Seth..." She let his name dangle there, begging for more.

He had to lower his head for a minute and take a deep breath before he withdrew and took that achingly rich ride once again, ending ever deeper than before. She was so slick and so wet for him that each move was over too soon. Those pert little tits danced against his chest, making him dizzy with lust. He wanted all of her, all at once.

"Do it again, Seth," she breathed. "Slow."

He grinned "You like that."

"Love it," she half-groaned, arching her back, drawing him in. "Love everything with you."

That L-word was getting dangerously close to the *you*, and he wanted to hear more of it. Maybe even with the other words cut away.

He thrust again, deeper still. Her fingernails tightened on his shoulder, and he willed her to let the words slip. *Love you.* Because Jesus, he was close to blurting it himself.

He was also close to coming before she did, which just wouldn't do. They'd had a kind of silent competition about that before, each stubbornly clinging to the edge of climax, unwilling to be the first to go over the edge. Most of the time, it had been a tie. This time? He was absolutely not going to let this wall-scaling, bike-hopping, bullet-dodging woman show him up. No way.

His dick screamed for release as his hips rocked. His heart pounded. Slow and steady sped up to fast and furious, and everything was the rub of his cock inside her incredibly tight sheath, the feel of her fingers clamping hard on his back. Each thrust pulled a gratifying little whimper out of her until she was moaning his name and making him feel like he was a goddamn pirate with his prize — his highly willing and skilled prize. She knew just how to fire off those shockingly effective inner muscles so that a ripple passed over his dick just as he plunged through like a lion through a flaming ring.

He lost track of in and out, where he ended and she started. He just flew along for the ride until Julie convulsed around him

— once, twice, three times. She let out a keening cry just as he hit the same wall and finally shot his release into her.

He blazed into the whiteout of a dizzying high, followed by a warm, dreamy haze in which he sensed her body and the sea breeze and not a single other thing. Didn't want to. Didn't have to, because nothing else mattered.

Something tickled his cheek. Her lips. Her weight shifted and he eased her down slowly, not wanting to break the magic. Wanting it to go on forever like some kind of never-never land.

And it might have, if she hadn't whispered in his ear.

"What's that sound, Seth?"

The sound of his heart, tapping out love songs in his chest?

"What sound?"

She angled her head toward the open sea, where the sound of the waves was broken by a distant buzz.

"That sound."

His ears caught it then, and every muscle that had just been busy melting away into bliss jumped back to attention. Because that sound was a motorboat, and it was coming toward them.

Chapter Fifteen

Seth didn't get the second half of his pirate fantasy, not with the sound of a throaty, powerful engine approaching the island at full speed. In the moonlight, the hull was only a dim silhouette, but it was there, all right — the low, sleek form of a motorboat.

"Shit." Seth looked at *Serendipity*. He'd told Tobin to leave the anchor light off, but the glow of the cabin lights could be seen a mile away.

He felt Julie's hand tighten around his forearm. "Um, a late arrival in the anchorage?"

"Could be." Even as he said it, he knew that wasn't the case.

"Fishing charter maybe?" she tried.

The distant roar became a quiet hum as the motorboat slowed and made a long, calculating curve one way, then another.

"Maybe," he said, though his gut said *Unlikely*. What kind of suicidal sea captain would run these reefs at night?

The kind of sea captain who knew these reefs like the back of his hand. One with a very good GPS unit and a very pressing reason for wanting into this anchorage. Right now.

Part of him wanted to hide on the island; the other part urged him to get back to *Serendipity*. Home. Safety in numbers, if his brother could be counted on to help in a pinch.

If.

"Let's get going." Seth made sure it came out calm and easy, but there was no mistaking his rush in grabbing his clothes and heading to the dinghy.

Julie was quick and quiet in doing the same, though she stopped just before they pushed the dinghy away from shore. "I owe you missionary style on a coral beach, pirate." She pulled him into a hug and mumbled the rest. "And don't you forget it."

Even with his nerves white-knuckling at the prospect of who might be in that motorboat, his soul soared. "Promise?"

She gave a firm nod. "Promise."

They pushed off and hopped into the dinghy in unison. The moon rippled on the sea, glinting over the eastern horizon. Gliding over the water at night always felt like space flight to him, though tonight, he couldn't stop to revel in the beauty of it.

His mind spun. Was it a fishing boat out for an overnight charter? A drug runner? Worse, the men who were after Julie?

He wanted to reject the thought, but it just wouldn't let go. How would those men get out here? And how would they know where to find *Serendipity*? How could they even know she was on board?

By the time the dinghy bumped *Serendipity's* hull, his unease had grown. The motorboat was headed right for them. He cut the outboard engine, and in the quiet that ensued, he could hear his brother's voice.

"Yeah, it's nice and calm out here at Cayo Coco..." Tobin was saying into the radio.

Shit! Seth nearly climbed right over Julie in his haste to shut his brother up. This was no time to be broadcasting their position on the sailors' evening chat hour!

A powerful searchlight came on, catching Seth in midstep on the stern ladder.

"Hands up!" came a Spanish-accented voice through the night.

Julie blinked like a deer in headlights, and Seth froze, too.

"Hands up!" This time, the voice came with the metallic click-clack of a rifle being cocked.

His hands shot up. He could make out the outline of a thirty-foot boat and three heads. Or was it four? He had to do something — but what? Should he tell Tobin to hide?

Shove Julie overboard and create a distraction while she swam away? But there was nowhere to go. Nowhere to hide.

"Holy shit, what ass is coming this close—" Tobin came up the companionway ladder, then froze when the light swung to him.

The motorboat closed the distance slowly, a hunter closing in on its prey. It hummed in a slow semicircle around *Serendipity*, then approached from astern and slid alongside. Seth winced as the hull scraped *Serendipity's*.

"Hey, man, that paint job is new!" Tobin shouted, pushing at the motorboat's rail.

Seth shoved Julie behind him as a man jumped over *Serendipity's* lifelines and thumped onto the deck. With the spotlight backlighting him, it was impossible to make out his face but the gun in his hand was perfectly clear.

"*Señorita* Steffens, how nice to see you again," the man all but purred in his flowery Spanish accent.

Seth shifted his weight to the right, making a wall in front of Julie.

"Can't say the feeling's mutual," she shot back.

Seth reached a warning hand backward to find her waist and raised the other in front of him like a stop sign. "What do you want?" he demanded.

Another figure jumped aboard, making *Serendipity* lurch. The rubbing hulls make a nails-on-the-chalkboard screech that went right down his spine.

Intruder One flicked his gun toward the cabin. "Inside. All of you. Now."

Julie hesitated, but Seth nudged her toward the steps, keeping himself between the men and her body. The cabin was tiny, with a single, narrow aisle in the middle. He crowded Julie as far back as possible and stretched to full height. They stood there, three ducks in a row — Julie, up forward, him next, and Tobin closest to the intruders in the aft section of the cabin.

Tobin shot him a look that said, *Shit, what now?*

The best he could offer was a look that replied, *Stay cool.*

The leader had a thick mustache and wore a brown shirt, brown pants, and high boots that gave him a shady, mercenary look. And for all Seth know, that's what the man moonlighted as, even if the insignia of the Belize Defense Force graced his sleeve.

"*Señorita* Steffens, you have a package. I want it."

Tobin swung around, shooting Julie a wide-eyed look that said *Jesus, girl! Even I'm not stupid enough to transport other people's shit!*

Seth bristled at his brother. Julie wasn't stupid. She wouldn't do anything illegal. Would she?

"And who are you?" Julie stuck her chin out, showing more indignation than fear. Seth couldn't help but marvel at her one more time. His girl had balls.

His girl. He shifted to keep her covered as well as he could, given only his body as a shield.

"*Capitan* Hernandez of the Defense Force."

"And you're here in an official capacity?"

"Of course!" the man said, his voice going saccharine-sweet.

Yeah, right, Seth thought.

Julie pursed her lips. "All I have is a package from Professor Leeds for the Sisters of Mercy Convent in Matigúas," she said, crossing her arms.

"Yes, Professor Leeds and I are old... friends."

Seth figured the hesitation meant the two were old adversaries.

"I am happy to deliver the package for you," Hernandez continued with a crocodile smile.

"I bet," Julie shot back.

He made a tiny gesture with the gun and scowled. "What exactly would you like to bet, *señorita?*"

The cabin fell silent; even Tobin held his tongue. The rubbing hulls sounded rougher from belowdeck, and every ripple on the water brought a low groan from *Serendipity.* Seth took a deep breath. This was his grandfather's boat — the boat he'd been entrusted with. Couldn't he do better than this?

He took a step toward the intruder but stopped immediately when the gun barrel swung toward his chest.

He put his hands up. He loved this boat, but it wasn't worth his life. Wasn't worth Julie's safety.

"Give it to him," he said, leveling the man with a gaze that made it clear the gun was the only thing keeping him from closing in.

He didn't know what was in the package, but it wouldn't be a rosary, not with these goons after it. He nodded at Julie, urging her to hand it over. The sooner they were rid of whatever it was, the better.

She let a second tick by before reaching for her backpack and pulling out a shoebox-shaped package. In seething silence, she passed it to Seth. It weighed as much as a couple of pounds of flour. Substantial, but not leaden. Seemed to him that drugs would weigh more. He passed it to Tobin to give to the man and nearly made a shooing motion with his hands.

"It's yours," he said. *Whatever it is.* "Go." *Get the hell off my boat.*

The man lowered his gun — didn't need it, not with his buddy leaning down from the cockpit with a rifle trained right between Tobin's eyes — and weighed the package in his hand as a greedy smile stretched across his face.

"*Gracias, senorita.* Next time the good Professor Leeds asks you to transport something for him, you maybe think twice. Or—" he grinned broadly "—you bring it to me."

"Like there'll be a next time," Julie replied, her face pinched tight.

"*Adios,*" Tobin chipped in.

The man only smiled more broadly. "Oh, we're not finished yet." He motioned with his gun. "On your knees."

Chapter Sixteen

A cold shiver rippled down Seth's back.

Tobin put his hands up. "Hey man, you got what you wanted. Just take it and go! We didn't do anything."

There was a glint of steel and a blur of motion as the man smacked the barrel of his gun across Tobin's cheek. Tobin grunted and dropped like a stone; Julie let out a horrified squeak. Seth heard his own guttural shout of protest while the men leaning in from the cockpit roared like spectators at a boxing match.

Seth leaned over his brother, cussing under his breath before getting kicked away by the man with the gun. He tumbled backward, and the hand he held up to ward off whatever came next was covered in blood. His brother's blood.

"Fuck, man," Tobin muttered from the floor, cupping his cheek.

"On your knees!" the man shouted.

Tobin was already there; Julie folding to the floor. Seth threw a frosty look at the intruder before complying. Rapid-fire Spanish mixed with English ensued, and a second man advanced with something bristling in his hand. He yanked Tobin's hand away from his face and forced it behind his back, jamming his wrists together and wrapping something around them.

Cable ties, Seth registered. The man was tying Tobin up. Did that mean the three of them would be left tied up or tossed overboard to drown? The intruders didn't seem to know either, judging by the tone of the discussion.

Then the radio squawked with a static-laced voice. "*Serendipity, Serendipity,* this is *Bluegrass, Bluegrass.* You still there?"

Everyone froze, and the voice came on again.

"Serendipity, Seren—"

The closest man clubbed the radio with the butt of his gun, sending bits of metal and plastic flying.

Seth stared at the remains of his radio and growled. His brand new, four-figure radio, bought just for this trip.

The second man stepped over Tobin, shoved Seth down, and yanked his hands together. He had no choice but to comply; struggling only made the cable tie cut deeper into his skin.

The man turned to Julie next, and every instinct in Seth blazed. Kill man. Protect woman. Protect his home.

Julie's eyes were defiant, but her cheeks were pale. Christ, if they touched her...

The man pulled her to her feet and yanked her hands behind her back. Then he stopped with an appreciative cluck.

Julie paled, and a hundred ugly scenarios flashed through Seth's mind. He braced his right foot against the floor, collecting his body to spring off his knees and into action — any action.

The man brushed a hand down Julie's back then turned to his colleagues with a grin.

"Maybe we take a second prize tonight," he purred to the others.

Seth dipped his right shoulder down, ready to body check the man. What he'd do after that with his hands tied behind his back and three guns trained on him, he didn't know, but he wouldn't just stand there while they had their fun.

The man's left hand slid an inch lower. Lower, past the hem of her shorts. His right hand slid along Julie's waist.

Every muscle in Seth's body tensed as he prepared to spring. Not. Letting. That. Happen. Never. Every leaden thump of his heart was a vow.

Then a godawful crackling sound broke the still air, and all eyes swung toward the door. The radio on the police boat erupted into a harried mix of static and guttural shouts.

Seth's ears strained to make sense of the noise.

"Capitán! Capitán!" The man outside in the cockpit motioned at Hernandez. *"Capitán!"*

A jumble of Spanish followed, and even the man ogling Julie looked pained. Were they being called away on another mission — a legitimate one? Maybe getting called in to report?

Hernandez's eyes flashed, and he gripped his gun tighter as if squeezing off a couple of rounds might ease the frustration so evident in his face. His jaw clenched. *"Vamos."*

A stone rolled off Seth's heart. At least, that's what it felt like when the man next to Julie stepped back. He scowled, whipped a cable tie around Julie's wrists, and shoved her so hard, she went sprawling across the floor. Seth nearly did the body check then.

Cable-tie man stomped past, kneeing Seth in the ribs, punching Tobin's back. Seth struggled to stay upright as pain flooded his taut nerves — along with relief. The men were all stamping up the stairs. Away. Out.

"Senorita Steffens." Hernandez paused at the doorway, motioning with his gun.

Seth managed to lean right, blocking a clear shot at Julie. Just in case.

"I suggest you forget what happened here and get out of my country," Hernandez said. "Soon. Because remembering..." The man paused in his warning, tut-tutting with his head. "That would be bad. Very bad."

Out of the corner of his eye, Seth saw Julie roll to her back. Her lips were moving, formulating some clever reply, but she bit it back. Barely, judging by the angry twitch of her cheeks.

Then mustache man was gone, too, and multiple footsteps resounded through the hull. There was a thump, shouted orders, and the roar of the other boat's engine, followed by an ear-splitting scrape along the length of *Serendipity.*

The roar receded into the distance, and they were alone.

Alive.

Kicking, more or less.

The taste of bile filled his mouth as he imagined the alternative.

His eyes swung to his brother's blood-smeared face. Tobin twisted, then groaned and gave up.

"Julie," Tobin sighed at the ceiling, "you sure got some 'splaining to do."

Chapter Seventeen

"We need to get out of here first," Julie said, twisting her hands where they were bound behind her back.

Seth could see her contorting, trying to work her hands free. He figured it should be at around this point that the average woman — hell, the average man — would break into tears and collapse in a puddle on the floor. But Julie's eyes were flashing anger, not fear. She was flopping around like a fish on a line and muttering under her breath — a whole flood of expletives, all of them aimed at one man.

"Professor Fucking Gregory Leeds, when I get my hands on you," she started. With a roll and a heave, she flopped over to her stomach. "Sisters of Mercy Convent in Matigúas, my ass," she panted, wiggling into a tripod position with her forehead and two knees under her body, her butt in the air while her hands continued writhing behind her back.

"You'll only make it tighter," Seth warned, casting around for some sharp object. Too bad he ran a tight ship — there was nothing loose lying around. Not from his perspective on the floor, at least.

"We don't have much time." Julie grunted as she pushed herself up on her knees.

Seth didn't like the sound of that. But Tobin beat him to the question. "What do you mean, not much time?"

She shook her head and heaved to her feet, swaying there for a minute before blinking and taking a step aft. She started picking her way past Seth's sprawled limbs, then Tobin's as each of them struggled to sit up.

"They'll be back when they realize..." She trailed off.

"When they realize what?" Tobin barked.

Silverware clinked as she rooted around in the galley and cursed. "Tobin, tell me how close I am."

"You're changing the subject."

"I'm trying to find something to cut us free."

Smart girl. Seth nodded to his brother. Julie might not be able to see what she was reaching for, but Tobin could. "Come on, tell her."

"There's a knife on your left. No, my left. Wait, that way," Tobin started.

Seth could hear her sigh of exasperation. "Just tell me hot or cold."

"Cold. The other way. Warmer. Warmer..."

Seth heaved his body up, only to slam into the underside of the table built into the center of the cabin. Some pirate he made.

"Warmer," Tobin went on as the silverware continued to rattle. "Hot! Hot! There!"

"Got it," she said.

Seth tried standing up again, and this time, he made it to the seat beside the table. Julie, meanwhile, was turning around, then turning back, then facing forward again, trying to figure out how to work the knife in between her bound wrists. Her gaze flipped to Tobin and paused there for a moment, weighing her choices. Whether to hand him the knife and let him cut her free, or to use it to cut his first, maybe?

Another second's hesitation then she turned to Seth instead. His inner audience gave a little cheer.

"Here, take it," she said, shuffling over so she was back-to-back with him. "Got it?"

He lurched to his feet and let his fingers search around. Past the fabric of her khaki shorts, past the light cotton of her shirt — there. His fingers found hers and traced their way to the knife — the six-inch kitchen knife that badly needed sharpening. Great.

"Got it."

"Tobin, can you see? Tell him where to aim," she said.

"Move a little," Tobin started. "OK. Um, stick the knife, well, I mean, put it, I mean..."

"Tobin!" they both shouted at the same time.

"I can barely see your hands," he complained.

"How's that?" Julie asked, bending forward at the waist so that he had a clear view of the space behind her back. Seth knew because the motion shoved her perfect ass into his and sent a series of completely inappropriate images through his mind. But now was really not the time, so he forced himself to concentrate on the knife clutched awkwardly between his fingers.

Silence. Nothing. He looked toward Tobin and found him staring at Julie's long, lean legs and perfect ass.

"Tobin!" he barked.

"Right." Tobin blinked. "You need to get the tip in closer."

Seth clenched his jaw. "Closer where? I don't want to slit her wrists."

"With that knife?" Tobin scoffed. "It's way too dull."

"Great," Julie muttered.

He tried again, his fingers jittery with either numbness or fear. Whichever.

"Hey," she whispered, softer now. "Relax. I trust you."

It wasn't just the words. It was the tone, the way her body scooped alongside his. Julie, trusting him with her life.

Like his heart could pound any harder.

"Yeah, but do you trust him?" Seth tried joking it off by aiming an elbow toward his brother.

She cocked her head at Seth, locking her blue eyes on his. "Trust him? Mostly. Now get to work, captain."

It took three minutes — and decade off his lifespan, Seth figured — but he did it. Got the knife behind the cable tie, sawed away from her until he heard an audible snap. He froze, waiting for a warm trickle of blood to signal he'd missed badly, but there was only a happy squeak and a flutter as Julie's hands flew up. She was free.

Seth blew out a long, grateful breath. He wished he could see her face. Wished he could hug her. Wished. . .

Her hands were already on his, the blade slipping easily into place, reminding him there was no wishing, only action.

Another snap, and his hands were free, too. His moment to spin around and face her.

But Julie was already stepping over to Tobin.

"Cut me, baby," his brother joked. Even with a bloody face, the guy was a charmer. Julie didn't even crack a smile, a woman on a mission.

Then Tobin was free, too, and Julie was climbing up the steps to the cockpit.

"The coast is clear," she announced. The second part was quieter. "For now."

What did she mean, for now?

"Julie, what's going on?"

Chapter Eighteen

What was going on? Julie leaned her elbows on the edge of the cockpit, staring out over the sea. Part of her was keeping lookout, but the other part was ready to dry heave, and not from seasickness. She'd been such a fool.

If I can ask you for one more favor before you go, my dear? The professor had looked so honest, so sincere when he said it.

Sure. Anything, she'd stupidly replied.

I have a gift and some documents for an orphanage we support in Matigúas. The post is so unreliable, you know. And since you're heading that way...

He might as well have added, *And since you're such a trusting idiot, you'll smuggle this package over an international border for me.*

She'd figured he had some scam going, old Professor Leeds. But something small-time, as it seemed just about every second person in Guatemala did. His jeep was much too new, his accommodations near the excavation site flashier than anyone else's. The place had a pool, for Christ's sake!

Drive carefully, my dear.

She should have read the subtext: *Watch that the corrupt cops don't run you down then chase you out to sea. 'Cause you'll be on your own then, my dear.*

But she wasn't alone. That was the one good thing about all this. Some kind fate had brought her Seth.

Seth, who was stepping up to her now, running a calming hand over her back when he could have been screaming for answers.

God, what had she done? Not only had she stumbled into hot water, she'd dragged Seth into this, too. He'd terrified her even more than that jerk who'd fondled her ass and suggested to his comrades that they stop for a little fun. Seth had started bristling like a papa bear, growling and flashing the evil eye that promised hell and beyond if they touched her. Even from his trussed-up position on the floor, she swore Seth looked twice his usual size. Big and bristly and lethal in that don't-fuck-with-my-woman kind of alpha male way.

If he had jumped the intruders, they would have shot Seth dead. His heroics would have been for nothing. If it hadn't have been for the radio calling the cops away... She shivered, trying not to imagine her own rape. His murder. The horrible end.

Another set of feet joined them on deck. Tobin. He'd been in danger, too, and had a gun smashed across his face. He could have lost an eye — or worse.

"This is all my fault." Her head was hanging so low, she could barely hear her own voice.

"No, it's my idiot brother's," Seth said. "He's the one who announced our position to everyone in radioland."

She heard Tobin sink into the seat behind her. "I know." His voice was distant, hollow. It didn't sound like the first time the brothers had been through that exchange.

Funny how they each played a role — so perfectly that she doubted they were even aware of it. Seth was the responsible older brother who did all the right things. Tobin was the rebel, the party boy, the carefree surfer — the one who could be counted on to make mistakes. Then along came this boat and knocked them out of their little worlds. Tobin could take some real responsibility while Seth could loosen up.

Back home, she'd never have fallen for a guy like Seth. But out here, in sailor mode, the appeal of a man in transition toward something better was hard to resist. She wanted to smooth the last city edges off him like the sea works on a pebble, rolling it over and over until it was round.

Except he'd ditched her two months back, right?

Her heart gave a little twinge underneath her ribs. He hadn't ditched her. Not exactly. She had pinned the blame on him too quickly. A little like Seth was doing with Tobin now, when it wasn't Tobin's fault.

She straightened her back and sat up to face them. "No, it's my fault." She put a finger under Tobin's chin and tipped his bloody face up. "My fault." God, she hated those words. Didn't have much practice with them either. But it was true, and she had to live with it. "Someone must have seen me heading to *Serendipity,* and how hard could it be to guess where we went?"

A wave slapped the side of the boat — a reminder that they had to get going before Hernandez discovered what she'd done. "Anyway, I'll explain once we get going."

"Going? Where?"

She looked at the inky seascape. To the west lay the lights of the mainland. To the east, the dark splotch that was the little island. Beyond it, the silvery, rippling sea.

Where to go?

There was really only one choice, and that was straight into trouble.

Chapter Nineteen

Julie was still eyeing the mainland, a haunted look shadowing her face when Seth took her by the shoulders and turned her gently around.

"Julie, talk to me. Explain." He made sure it came out the way he meant it — a plea, not an order.

"Yeah, explaining would be good," Tobin added, not quite as diplomatically.

Seth watched her eyes slide to his brother, then wince. "Let's get you cleaned up first." Her shoulders lifted then fell in a deep breath.

They filed back into the cabin, where Seth pulled out the first aid kit while Julie turned a light on Tobin's cheek.

"Shit," Seth said. He knew it was bloody, but hell, his brother's wound was worse than he'd thought. Julie dabbed the blood away, revealing an inch-long gash and a purplish-red swelling the size of a fist.

"Not that bad," Tobin muttered, giving that lazy wave he specialized in. Except Seth didn't buy it, not one bit. Tobin's knuckles were white where his hands gripped the chart table and his back was uncharacteristically stiff. Seth looked his brother up and down, wondering how often Tobin had shown the world that same dismissive veneer when he had to be hurting inside. Wondered how he'd ever missed it before.

Shit, maybe his kid brother was more of a man than he gave him credit for.

Julie spread out the first aid supplies on the chart table then pushed back Tobin's hair to clean his cheek.

"Ouch," Tobin said, though he quickly drifted into that dreamy state that house cats get when curled on their favorite armchair. Getting petted. In the sun. Except Tobin's spot was nearly cheek to cheek with Seth's girl. Her body was so close, it was nearly brushing his.

A heat wave pulsed through Seth's veins. This was exactly why he hadn't invited her to the boat before. His brother had a way of charming more than just the proverbial pants off women, and even the smartest ones went all fluttery when they met him.

Julie obviously didn't do fluttery. She did serious. Smart.

And Julie was his, damn it! Not Tobin's. No way.

Sure, Seth got his fair share of interest from women, but they were rarely the kind of woman he was interested in. And for once, it felt good to be chosen in a direct comparison to his happy-go-lucky brother. The one who got everything so easily: girls, fun, crazy adventures.

Seth, on the other hand, got into good schools. Got promoted. But he never got to be just himself, except around her.

Julie liked his jokes. Julie had no fear. Well, hardly any. She could talk boats, sports, and politics. She'd seen the world, but when she looked into his eyes, it felt like everything else ceased to exist.

Including his brother, whom she'd never shown any interest in. Even now, she seemed immune to Tobin, concentrated entirely on patching him up. And Tobin had been remarkably hands off so far. Seth had to give him that.

Just in case, though, he handed Julie the bottle of antiseptic and motioned toward his brother's face.

Tobin caught a whiff of it and leaned back. Way back. "Shit, that's gonna sting."

"Don't want it to get infected," Seth said. Which was technically true.

Tobin made a hissing noise when Julie dabbed it on, and she started speaking so quietly, Seth almost missed her first words.

"The man in charge of the Xtlemacán excavation site — Leeds — gave me some documents to deliver. Stupid, I know." Her voice was all anger and no self-pity. "But after getting chased, I figured something was up. So I looked in the package."

The cabin went still until Tobin spoke up. "And?"

"There was a box inside the box."

"So what was in it?"

"I don't know." She started unpeeling sticky sutures and lining them up over Tobin's gash. "I mean, I know, but I don't know what it's for."

"What what's for?" Tobin mumbled out the side of his mouth.

"And what's the rush to get out of here? They have what they want." Seth waved a hand west, where the motorboat had gone.

"No, they don't." She stuck on a last suture and leaned back to examine her work then gave a little nod.

"Julie!" Tobin forced her to meet his gaze just on the strength of his voice. "Explain."

She bit her lip and started studying the floor. "I took the inner box out. Filled the outer box with about the same weight of stuff." She glanced up with a rueful expression. "I owe you a couple of paperbacks."

So that's why she'd taken so long before dinner. Then a realization clicked in Seth's mind.

"Not the Patrick O'Brians!"

The look she gave him said, *Are you kidding?* "No, I took those smutty adventure books."

Tobin yelped. "Not my Caribbean pirate series!"

She gave a weak nod. "Sorry."

Tobin rushed to the forward cabin then rushed back, looking positively anguished. "There was a picture in one of those books. . ."

"I took out the notes and bookmarks and stuck them behind the shelf." Julie disappeared into the forward berth then backed out. "These?"

Tobin snatched the papers and held them to his chest, but not before Seth got a look at the top one — and did a double take.

"Jesus, man, you still have a picture of Cara? That was like five years ago!"

Tobin swung his body away to shield it. "Six," he mumbled then stalked forward to tuck the picture out of sight.

His brother was still pining for Cara? Seth thought Tobin was long since over the fiasco of his almost-wedding. But judging by the way Tobin looked at the photo now — holding it in two hands like his most precious possession... Maybe not. Considering how much it hurt to have lost Julie for two months... Seth didn't want to think what six years would be like.

Except that now was hardly the time for all that. He rocked on his heels, trying to piece together Julie's story. "So those goons have a couple of paperbacks and we have...what?"

"Where?" Tobin added.

Julie's eyes slid toward the bathroom cabinet between the main cabin and forward berth.

"Under there."

Seth was on his knees in a minute, pulling out fishing gear and spare parts.

"Stuck up by the sink drain," she whispered, so quietly you'd think she didn't want it found.

He groped around until his hand found a square corner among the curved pipes then followed it along the edges of a box. He worked it out of the tight space, then sat back on his heels, looking at it. A Marlboro carton, frayed around the edges. He turned it over and gave it a shake. Solid, by the feel of it. Not too heavy, not too light. "So what's in it?"

"Have a look," Julie sighed.

He brought it to the salon table and stared at the flap for a minute. Who stashed documents in a Marlboro carton? Who delivered things to convents that way?

"Open it already," Tobin urged.

Seth popped the end flap open, tipped the box, and shook it a little so the first sheaf of paper slid out.

For a minute, there was only a collective catching of breath, the distant murmur of waves on the beach. Then Tobin let out a long, appreciative whistle.

Seth leaned back.

Julie took a breath so deep, the air pressure in the cabin dropped. "There's more."

He shook the box again, mind spinning as he did. "How much more?" he asked as the next batch of greenbacks came edging out.

"Oh," she said, "about a hundred thousand dollars more."

Chapter Twenty

Seth had done his share of night sailing when he and Tobin brought the boat down the East Coast of the US to the Caribbean, but that was in open water. Navigating through reefs at night went against every sailor's rule of common sense. He could feel his grandfather's ghost peering over his shoulder as he started the engine and weighed anchor. Hand over hand, he pulled the chain up, every link a gritty reminder of why this was such a bad idea.

But staying was a bad idea, too. They'd been through the options and reluctantly agreed to Julie's plan. There was no better way.

He hauled up an arm's length of anchor chain and decided she was crazy. On the next length, he went back to thinking she was brilliant. Or maybe just a combination of the two. His thoughts seesawed that way through another eighty feet of chain.

"Anchor up!" he called back to Tobin, who stood at the wheel. Julie was below, eyeing their GPS, calling out instructions to the helm as they backtracked over their exact inbound track. Slowly. Very slowly. Seth stayed at the bow as lookout, though the only reefs he could make out in the light of the moon were dull underwater shadows that were only clear when they appeared directly under the bow — much too late to call a warning. So far, they'd been lucky.

So far.

His mind spun over the possibilities one more time.

They couldn't go to the police, because the men who'd pointed guns at them less than an hour ago were cops. Corrupt cops, from the look of it.

They couldn't dispose of the cash or simply keep it, as Tobin suggested. Dirty cash was dirty cash, whether it came from the illegal sale of illicit artifacts or drugs — and getting rid of it or running wouldn't get the corrupt cops off their backs. Then there was the source: when Professor Leeds found out his package never made it, he'd come after *Serendipity*, too.

"But a boat is a boat," Seth tried. "We can always take off for Mexico or Honduras."

"Yeah," Tobin said skeptically. "All those not-at-all corrupt places. We can add Panama to the list. Maybe go to Colombia."

Point made. And anyway, they'd never outrace the motorboat if it decided to take up the chase.

They couldn't accept Julie's original suggestion, either: that since it was all her fault and she was such an idiot — her words — they ought to dump her at the nearest port and let her deal with it on her own.

Right. Like he'd ever let that happen. Hell, he'd had the woman up against a tree at the beginning of this crazy night. And the secret promise he'd made then — that he'd do anything to convince her to give him one more chance — was one he'd never break.

But to get to the point where they could even think about that, they had to get rid of the cash in a way that got the cops off their tail. But how?

Serendipity nosed out of the lee of the island and into open water. It was a relatively calm night with a steady trade-wind breeze. That much, at least, was on their side for what they had in mind.

They'd need any luck they could get, because the trickiest option was the last one — the one they were heading for like three blind mice.

Chapter Twenty-One

Julie kept her eyes on the GPS and her hands gripped tightly along the sides of the chart table. All those reefs and a very thin, meandering line to follow between them — at night. And it wasn't like *Serendipity* had headlights; all they had was the light of the moon. Seth had even turned off the mast-top light and taken down the radar reflector to make it harder for Hernandez and his men to find *Serendipity* when they realized they'd been duped. Which probably wouldn't take long.

The electronics console in front of her had a busted radio. Tobin, steering at the boat's wheel, had a busted cheek, because of her. Seth, keeping lookout at the bow, had a fire in his eyes that scared her with its intensity. And Julie, she had a busted ego. She'd messed up — no, fucked up — big-time. She'd caused all this.

"A little more to the right," she called out the cabin door.

"Starboard," Tobin called back quietly, his voice light and patient. Which only made her hang her head lower. She'd never taken the younger brother seriously, but the man had the heart of a soldier, the courage of a lion. He had no reason to help her on this at all — but he was all in. Unquestioningly on her team.

God, she'd lucked out with these two. Especially with Seth. How had she ever doubted him?

Well, she'd bury her head in a bucket later — if Hernandez and his men didn't do that for her. Right now, she had to focus on guiding the boat out of the reefs, then getting to the convent.

Which was probably going to be about as safe as sailing a boat through a maze of reefs at night. But she was sure that was the only way. Professor Leeds wanted the package delivered to the convent at Matigúas? He'd get it delivered.

"But are the nuns really nuns?" Seth had made a good point when they hashed it out.

"There was a name on the package," she said. "A man's name. Roberto somebody. So I'm guessing the nuns are legit."

The more she thought about it, the more she decided the convent and orphanage really were legitimate. Professor Leeds had pictures of it all over the excavation office — lots of shots of happy kids giving the camera a thumbs-up. News article clippings, even. If Leeds was using the convent, it was as a front.

"I don't get it. Why is an archaeologist sending money to a convent?" Seth had asked.

She shrugged. "I bet he's selling artifacts illegally in Guatemala then laundering the money through Belize. I bet part of it really does get to the nuns and the kids. But the rest probably goes to a private account. And this guy Roberto, I figure, is Leeds' inside man."

"A guy in a convent?"

"A gardener, maybe," she guessed. "The rector? Who knows? Just someone to handle Leeds' payments without drawing attention to himself."

"Let's hope Roberto isn't the guy who buries bodies in the yard," Tobin had muttered then.

In the end, they decided it didn't matter — much. If they could get the money to the nuns, it would be off their hands. There'd be no evidence of wrongdoing on their part, and Professor Leeds, if he had his own band of goons, couldn't reprimand her for delivering the package as requested. Right?

"Unless the convent turns out to be a drug den," Seth pointed out. "Then we're completely screwed."

They would be screwed. Her logic was shaky at best, the whole plan a long shot. Julie chewed her lips and plucked at a strand of her shirt as her eyes strained at the GPS screen. No need to get ahead of herself. Right now, getting back to the mainland was all that mattered.

"A little more lef— port," she called.

"A born sailor," Tobin chuckled. Humor in the line of fire — the man had guts.

She eyed the distance to the mainland on the chart. Twenty miles. Didn't seem like much, but Seth said it would take about four hours.

"Except the damn tide's against us," Tobin muttered.

Right, the tide. She eyed the navigation instruments uncertainly. Some pirate she'd make.

Seth, on the other hand, made a damn good buccaneer. Scruffy hair, shadowed chin, dark eyes. The couple of times he ducked into the cabin to check the instruments, he could have had a knife between his teeth and said *Arrr, arrr!* When he checked with Tobin at the wheel, his commands were curt and confident, as if he'd been piloting these waters all his life.

That second chance he'd been talking about — she wanted it, too. If they ever got out of this mess.

It took five hours in the end, and her eyes were dry and scratchy by the time they dropped anchor in a secluded cove not far south of Santa Marta. The place didn't even appear on the chart, just as a sketch on the back of a beer coaster another sailor had given Seth some time ago. He had a whole collection of them — navigation coasters, he called them with a little grin.

When Julie finally left the chart table to come on deck, the sky was split into a dozen layers of pink, orange, and red.

"Wow," she breathed. Sunrise over the ocean was even more beautiful when seen from a boat, the water all around *Serendipity* turning gold.

It would have been a Kodak moment if she hadn't had so much on her mind. Then an arm slipped around her waist, and Seth was there, leaning his head against hers, giving her silent reassurance. The fringing jungle was alive with avian squawks and whistles, and the moon hung just above it, as if it had been waiting for them to wave it good day. A moment she didn't need a camera for to remember forever.

She sighed, and he did too. If only they could hide beneath a blanket and push the world away. But the sun was rising; it was time to get moving.

"Okay, Indiana Jones, you lead the way," Tobin said once they'd beached the dinghy and faced a thick wall of jungle.

She looked left, then right. The coastal road wasn't far inland, but getting there... She reached over a shoulder and withdrew her machete from its straps on the outside of her backpack, then glanced at Seth one more time.

He was gazing back at *Serendipity*, anchored so serenely in the cove, its reflection rippling slightly in the calm water. Then he caught her gaze and she saw it: a vision of the two of them on that boat, in another cove, another day. With all the serenity and none of the anxiety.

She took a deep breath and stilled her wobbly knees. Mission first. Future later.

Zing! She slashed the machete through the knotted undergrowth. *Swish!* A clutch of vines fell. *Whoosh!* Leaves the size of umbrellas fluttered to her feet. Given a couple of days, Mother Nature would work her magic, closing the gap like it had never been there.

Thwack! Step by step, she led her little band forward. There was a certain thrill to it, a high. And even though sweat was pouring down her face and her arm aching by the time they broke out onto the road, it felt good to be doing something other than running away.

"Now what?" Seth asked, looking up the empty road.

She wiped the sleeve of her T-shirt over her face. "We catch the first bus that comes along, get the bike, and hightail it to the convent." She patted the bulge in her backpack, feeling the package they couldn't wait to get rid of.

"Easy," she finished, hoping she was right.

Chapter Twenty-Two

An hour later, Julie was humming down the road on her motorcycle, street dust sticking to her sweaty skin. The bus driver had given her directions to the convent, twenty miles up into the hills, when he'd left them a few blocks from the place she and Seth had stashed her bike before fleeing for the boat.

Everything was a rush except getting on the bike, because the place she'd hidden it — in the bushes beside the beach bungalow where she'd been staying when she first met Seth — was full of memories. She could have stood there and relived them all day: the laughs, the late-night talks, the early-morning sex, and well... pretty much everything in between. Amazing how two people could tumble right into love, given the right time and place. She'd been scared to use the word then, but it was getting closer and closer to the tip of her tongue with every minute she spent with Seth.

Every minute, and every mile. Because they'd covered a hell of a lot already — on foot, by road, and on the boat. Hell, what an adventure.

When she shook herself out of her reverie and onto the bike and Seth swung up to sit behind her, that L word was closer than ever. The bumps in the road nearly rattled it out of her, as did the beauty of the morning sun, slanting gold-green over the fields and patchy forests along the way. It was quite the contrast to a night of sashaying gracefully over the ocean waves on *Serendipity*. And quite the contrast to her usual mode of travel — alone.

Seth's arms wrapped so far around her that they overlapped at her waist. He wasn't just hanging on. He was protecting, promising. If the Kawasaki's engine weren't so loud, she might even have said it.

I love you.

She pulled in a deep breath, letting her ribs expand under his touch. It was just the two of them, because they'd left Tobin in town. Assuming everything went smoothly, they would meet back at the beach bar later. A big assumption... But if things did pan out, she'd have a hell of a lot to say to Seth the minute she got the chance. Starting with those three words and *I want a chance with you, too.*

The hill was getting steeper and the truck in front of them slower, so she glanced at the triple image in the cracked side mirror.

The road was clear. She sped past the truck then pulled back into the right lane. A red car behind them did the same, and again when they both overtook a straining little three-wheeler piled high with fuel jugs. When the red car revved up to pass the next car, too, she looked more closely. And when it swung into the sharp right turn to the convent at the same time as her, she muttered out loud.

"Shit."

It was impossible to make out the driver's face with the shadows flitting across the road, but the colors of the license plate were clear enough. Not Belize's black-on-white, but the bright-blue-on-white of a Guatemala plate.

Shit, shit, shit.

She revved the bike so high, Seth nearly squeezed the air out of her to keep from tumbling off the back.

"What?" he shouted over the engine noise.

She dipped her chin toward the mirror. "Leeds, or one of his men."

She felt the weight shift as Seth twisted to look behind

"The cops, too!" he shouted.

What? She looked in the mirror again and cursed. The red car filled most of the crooked panes, but in the distance were a couple of jeeps, showing in triplicate. Everyone was closing in.

"Faster!" Seth urged, and she opened the throttle up.

The convent was a smudge of white at the end of a long green tunnel of magnificent banyan trees. A view she would have stopped at admire, if only she had the time. Instead, she swerved around an overhanging vine and sped on, eyeing the road where it narrowed ahead.

A minute later, she understood why. There was a stream and a tiny one-lane bridge ahead, forming a bottleneck.

"What now?" Seth uttered as she slowed down.

She pointed with an elbow. "It gets worse."

Seth, to his credit, didn't say the obvious: *How can it get worse?*

"They're fixing the bridge," she finished.

Even from a distance, she could see that the surface of the bridge was rutted and dotted with stacks of cobblestones waiting to be laid. A man walked toward the bridge from one side, leading a mule piled high with bamboo. Half a dozen men stood, kneeled, or hammered on the bridge, and a sign with a crooked arrow pointed left.

"What does *Desvio* mean?" Seth shouted into her ear.

"Detour."

He cursed. "Like we have time for a detour."

Definitely not. But maybe...

"Hang on," she yelled to Seth.

Six faces looked up from the bridge.

"Watch out!" she yelled.

"Juli—" Seth started, and one of the men jumped to his feet, waving his arms wildly to shoo her away.

She beeped. No time for a detour.

"Whoa!" Seth yelled and held on tighter.

She slowed down just enough to swerve around the detour sign then rev onto the upswing of the bridge. It was a lovely, cobblestoned arch that must have dated to colonial times, like the convent.

The vehicles in pursuit honked their horns as shouts rang out, and the mule brayed.

"Watch out!" she shouted, unwilling to let go of the handlebars now. "Get out of the way!"

Bodies leaped out of the way as she slalomed left around a pile of stones, then right around an openmouthed worker. If Seth hadn't thrown out his foot for balance, they might have wiped out when she twisted away from a gaping hole that appeared out of nowhere. *Bump, bump, bump—* the bike hammered over the stone path as a screeching sound of slamming brakes came from behind. The cars were stopping, unable to cross.

"Go! Go!" Seth shouted as she rolled the motorcycle down the other side of the bridge and lurched back onto the road.

There was more beeping and cursing, but at least there was no gunfire. Yet.

Her body gave a sigh of relief at the relative smoothness of the dirt road — smooth enough for her to peek in the mirror and see Professor Leeds gesticulating over the bridge. Apparently he'd gotten word that his $200,000 delivery hadn't made it to its destination on time.

"How far you reckon the detour will go?" Seth shouted.

She prayed it was far enough.

All her focus was on the whitewashed wall of the convent, an imposing colonial-era building that was as graceful as it was decayed. Chunks of plaster were flaking off the walls, and for every roof tile that lay in place, three others were crooked or missing entirely. There was something proud about the place though, too, like an aging diva who knew just what a beauty she'd once been.

Julie revved right up to the entrance and looked up. There was a grand archway with a bell tower and a cross, and though they needed every second of lead they had, it didn't feel quite right to drive into the courtyard at full speed, so she eased off the throttle and let the bike coast in.

Sun — shade — sun. The light flickered as they passed under the archway, then halted in the courtyard within.

"Wow," Seth mumbled over her shoulder.

Wow, indeed. It was the quintessential cloister courtyard, quartered into tidy flower beds that radiated from a bubbling stone fountain in the center. A dozen heads turned their way, little dots of white popping up from among the rainbow of flowers that graced the central garden. The nuns were at work in their Garden of Eden — or had been, until she'd roared in on the bike.

Julie gulped. When she cut the engine, there was silence, then a sudden chorus of birds. The nuns, however, just stared. If she could have melted away then, she would have, because now she and Seth were the intruders, the ones breaking the peace.

Seth slid off the seat and she followed suit, pulling off her helmet then hanging it on a handlebar of the bike.

"Now what?" Seth whispered.

With a loud crack, the helmet dropped, and the nun walking toward them scowled.

"Now we find the head, um, nun. Sister. Mother. Whatever they call her." Julie stepped forward, trying to steady the thumping of her heart. *"Buenos días,"* she started, trying to paste a smile on her face.

Chapter Twenty-Three

Seth looked on as Julie jabbered at the nun in Spanish. His back was still hunched from the rough ride, his ass was still burning from the bumps, and his balls, well... He shoved that thought away. They were in a convent, after all.

And he could feel it, too, because while the nuns regarded Julie as a curiosity from the modern world they had cloistered themselves away from, the looks they shot at him were more guarded, even hostile. He was most definitely not welcome here.

But Julie was doing that earnest head-dipping body language thing she did when she was really, really sorry about something. The way she gestured with her hands and fired off a hundred Spanish words a minute, he'd have pegged her as a local if it weren't for her fair complexion and straw-colored hair.

The nun looked from Julie to him in open suspicion, and there was a silent moment of truth. A second ticked by, then another, each marked by the slow slide of sweat down his back.

"Bueno." The nun nodded, motioned with an outstretched arm, and led them toward one of the archways surrounding the courtyard. Julie followed right on the woman's heels, so close she nearly stepped on the woman's habit. Seth put a hand on her shoulder. If there was one thing he'd learned about Central America, it was that you couldn't hurry anyone up.

Not even with a band of bad guys closing in? Julie's eyes seemed to ask.

He wavered for a second there. Those eyes were beautiful, hopeful, honest. He could wake up to them every day for the rest of his life if this somehow worked out.

If.

When they ducked into the shade of the breezeway, the temperature immediately dropped ten degrees. The distant rumble of engines faded as they stepped through a door and entered the building.

Stepping over the threshold was like crossing a time portal; he could have been stepping into the seventeenth century. Their feet scuffed across a stone floor. Their footsteps echoed through muted halls where shadow and light flickered in an endless wrestling match. Time hung in layers so thick, it blanketed the air like a heavy tapestry. Seth sensed it right away: this was a place of refuge. A contemplative place, where a man could think.

Like about how likely his ass was to land in a Central American prison by the end of the day. He could imagine his mother wringing her hands, wondering where her son had gone wrong.

"Por aquí," the nun said, leading them up a wide wooden staircase supported by thick beams. The whole place whispered of history and tradition. Maybe even a few ghosts, snooping from the shadows. Then they were upstairs, and she knocked urgently on a door. *"Hermana Christina?"*

Their panting breath was the loudest thing in the hallway as they waited for an answer. Then the nun held up a finger and disappeared inside.

Seth watched Julie watching him, knowing her cool exterior was just as much an act as his. He gave her a weak smile, lifted a hand to her cheek, and slowly traced the line of her jaw. His lips moved, though he couldn't quite get any words to come out. So much to say, no time to say it.

Her eyes shone in his. *I know what you mean.*

The door creaked open and he jerked his hand away.

"Come on in," came a gritty American voice he would never have associated with a nun. The first woman left them without a word, moving soundlessly down the stairs.

"Um, hello?" Julie said, leading the way inside.

Everything in the room was just as he'd imagined the head office at a convent to be: heavy curtains, oversized crucifix, vanilla-scented candles. Everything but the woman rising from a creaky chair to meet them.

"Come. Sit. Explain." She gestured and spoke at the same time. If she'd been chewing a wad of gum, she'd have been the spitting image of a beefy Brooklyn waitress. He could hear it in her accent. *Siddown. Have a cuppa caw-ffee.*

"I'm the head here, Sister Christine. And who are you?" She folded her arms across her habit. Seth would have pegged her as a truck driver, an inner-city school principal, a short-order cook in a very busy diner. Anything but a nun.

"Um, I'm Julie, and this is Seth, and we're here... I mean, um..."

The nun must have decided she liked Julie, because she smiled and extended a hand. "Let's start again. I'm Christine Madeleine Kelly, from New York." *New-Yawk.* "At least I used to be. Thirty years ago I came here because the big city wasn't big enough for a girl like me." She winked. She actually winked.

"I'm sorry," Julie started. "I mean, we're in trouble, and I don't want to bring it to you..."

"But?" The nun raised an eyebrow.

Julie looked at him for help, but damned if he could explain this any better than she. "It kind of got out of control."

As if to illustrate her point, brakes squealed outside, followed by the thump of car doors. A host of angry male voices carried up through the window.

Sister Christine's eyes flicked to the window, then back to Julie. Seth felt very much a side character on a female-dominated stage.

"Life has a way of doing that," she said, still studying Julie's face as if she could judge the truth just by looking long and hard enough. "So what exactly brings you here?"

"Well..." Julie started, rummaging in the backpack. Seth could tell she was trying to stay cool even as her hand worked frantically. "I worked with Professor Leeds in Guatemala, and he gave me this to deliver here."

Seth admired the way she worded it. *Deliver here.* No word of Roberto, the man the package had been addressed to.

"Gregory Leeds?" Christine raised a wary eyebrow.

The voices were closer now, rushing through the hallway downstairs. Seth could hear the thump of boots over stone as they approached.

Christine glanced at the door, then back at Julie. "I suspect we won't have time to get better acquainted," she said. Her gaze traveled up and down Julie's light frame, and she squeezed her lips together. "Pity, really. But it seems there's some kind of hurry."

Footsteps — heavy footsteps — were already crashing up the stairs.

Sister Christine threw her shoulders back, looking every inch a queen. *Just let them try to mess with me,* her whole body said.

Seth stepped closer to Julie, ready for a fight.

Chapter Twenty-Four

The door flew open and a man Seth immediately pegged as Professor Leeds stumbled in. He had that tweedy, academic look even if he wasn't actually wearing tweed. The man immediately caught himself and straightened his tie as if he'd been led in by a butler and not let himself in.

Hernandez was right on his heels and immediately pinned Seth with his piercing eyes. Flanking them were several other men. The cops were the beefy ones dressed in brown who deferred to Hernandez and wouldn't stop crossing themselves. Leeds' gang was slightly less hulking, but more calculating in the glances they shot toward the furniture and antiques filling the room, as if they'd stumbled into a gold mine.

Leeds and Julie eyed each other like a couple of wary copperheads, while the others looked on, vultures at ringside. Then a man dressed in gardening garb pushed himself past the others, started jabbering in apologetic tones to the head nun.

Sister Christine waved an unimpressed hand, and when she opened her mouth to speak, the room fell silent. Like that.

The only part Seth understood when Sister Christine chastised the gardener in Spanish was his name, Roberto. The one the package had been addressed to.

Oh, shit.

Then the nun switched to English — whether to keep the others off-balance or for his benefit, Seth couldn't tell. But Roberto slunk back behind the others, his eyes shooting daggers at Julie and Seth.

"Gentlemen," Sister Christine began.

Julie's eyes flashed at the word *gentlemen*, and Seth had to agree. *Gentlemen* was a stretch for these thieves. Hernandez and Leeds eyed each other like familiar adversaries that had been gambling at the same table for years. Seth imagined Leeds smuggling something under Hernandez's nose one time then taking a misstep and having his money or an artifact confiscated. Not that Hernandez would turn it in. No, he'd turn his own profit on the artifacts and let Leeds go so the next round could begin. Cat and mouse. Predator and prey. Sometimes one won, sometimes the other. Either way, someone stood to profit.

Sister Christine stared down the intruders until everyone drew half a step back.

"My dear Leeds, always a pleasure to see you," she said in a dry tone. She held a hand out to Julie, who handed her the Marlboro box. "What I don't understand is why you'd burden your student here with a package when you could have delivered it yourself."

"When I heard the gift wasn't delivered, I thought I'd come check on you," he babbled. "The roads can be so dangerous, my dear."

The good Sister huffed. "She looks perfectly capable to me."

Yeah, the nun was definitely not on Leeds' side. More like closing ranks with Julie in a show of female solidarity.

She started to pop the box open and Leeds made a pained sound. He stepped forward. "There's been a mistake."

Sister Christine lifted her eyebrows and fixed him with a look that said, *I dare you to go on,* and he froze. Her finger was under the end flap of the box, easing it open.

"A mistake?" She arched an eyebrow then looked inside the box. Her eyes lit, not with surprise or fear, but recognition.

Seth knew there and then that Leeds had met his match. Sister Christine was bold, brassy, confident. She'd obviously been around long enough to know the score. Her gaze picked Roberto out from the back of the crowd, and Seth watched him shrink away. Yep, she knew the score exactly.

Did she know that Leeds was involved in illegal trade of antiquities and that Roberto was his funnel? Probably. But there were worse crimes in the jungle, other battles to fight. If Leeds made regular donations to the convent's causes, what did it matter to the nuns if minor crimes slipped by?

Sister Christine shook the first bundles of American cash out the box without batting an eye. Her hand, though, went to her chest in an exaggerated display of surprise. "Oh! Professor Leeds! What on earth is this?"

She shook a little more and the rest of the money tumbled out, coming to rest in a green heap, right next to the beaded rosary on her desk.

The greenbacks reflected in the lenses of the professor's wire-rimmed glasses. "It's... er... Madame, that is meant to be—" He shot Julie a look that squealed, *What have you done?*

Julie played dumb. "It's a donation, right?"

The policemen leaned forward as one, all ears.

"Donation?" Leeds looked panicked.

"Your donation," Julie cued. "To the orphanage."

Leeds froze, chewed his lip, and looked desperately around the room. Hernandez and his cronies all but growled. His men were no help, keeping their eyes on the floor. The professor's thin shoulders slumped as he muttered, "Oh, that donation."

"We're delighted, of course!" Sister Christine fluttered her eyelids like a woman half her age, then repeated her words in Spanish to the handful of nuns peeking through the doorway.

"Bless you, Gregory Leeds!" Christine announced.

The nuns chimed in like so many chirping pigeons. "*Gracias, Senor* Leeds!" A half-dozen habit-framed faces bobbed.

"The children in the orphanage will be so grateful! The convent! The bishop, too."

Right on cue, the sounds of joyous children came bounding through the windows. Seth glanced outside, past the perimeter wall of the convent to where a couple dozen kids came pouring out of a small schoolhouse. From the look of things, recess was on. For a moment, he wondered if there was such a thing as holy intervention, but Sister Christine was just as likely to have a little red button wired to the underside of her desk. Right next to where she kept a shotgun. He wouldn't put either past her.

Sister Christine glanced over and winked.

Leeds mopped his dripping brow with a handkerchief. "The bishop?"

"For your donation, brought to us by this wonderful associate of yours!" Sister Christine gushed. She had a gleam in her eye, like this was the best fun she'd had since leaving New York.

Which was all fine, but what about the cops? Seth knew that bulge under Hernandez's jacket wasn't a badge.

Christine, however, seemed completely unfazed.

"And you, my dear *Capitán* Hernandez, you've come to make sure it arrived safely, yes?"

Hernandez stood stiff as a statue, but he managed a cold smile. "Of course."

"I can only imagine what your superiors will have to say when I tell them of your hard work."

There was a warning coded in those words, Seth could tell. *I know what game you're playing,* she was saying, *and I can blow the whistle any time I like.*

Hernandez's hand shot up. "That won't be necessary."

The nun flashed a huge smile. She'd played the situation just right, and she knew it. Julie looked at her in awe. Seth, too.

"Well, this is just wonderful. Wonderful!" Sister Christine clapped and turned to Julie. "My dear, I would love to thank you properly, but I know what a hurry you're in."

Julie looked a little lost. *Hurry?*

Then Seth got it and grabbed her elbow. "Yes, we're in a terrible hurry."

"Such a pity," the nun said.

"Really a pity," Seth parroted and took a side step toward the door.

Hernandez tensed, as if to block the way, but froze when Sister Christine barked an order.

"You!" Everyone went still as Sister Christine stared the men down. "The rest of you, I'll be delighted to invite for tea." She clapped and called through the door before they could protest. "*Hermana Maria!* Tea for these gentlemen, please!"

"Oh, I really couldn't accept," Leeds started.

"My dear professor, I insist." She nailed him with her words, and Seth knew he was a goner. "A donation like this cannot go unacknowledged. And *Capitán* Hernandez!" she shouted, just as he was leaning toward Julie. The man jerked back like a puppet on a string. "You and your hard-working men must be famished. You'll join us, of course."

"Of course," he mumbled through tight lips.

"Yes, we'll all share tea. Then prayers."

If Seth were one of the men pulled into the net, he'd have groaned. As it was, a few of them were crossing themselves. But he and Julie, well, they took one last grateful look at Sister Christine, then did a walk-sprint straight out the door. A minute later, they were blinking in the tropical sunlight and making for the bike. He swung on behind her and circled his arms around her, good and tight.

Vroom! Julie roared out of the courtyard, under the arched entrance, and out — into their freedom.

"Holy..." Seth started, trying to digest everything that just happened.

He could see Julie grinning in the mirror. "Holy something is right. But you know what?" she shouted over the engine noise.

"What?"

"I think it's time to sail into the sunset. Just in case."

Epilogue

One day later in Pueblita, twenty miles south...

"You sure about this, man?"

Julie watched Seth study his brother, working his jaw a little before he said it again. "I mean, are you really sure?"

Tobin, in contrast, was wearing one of his trademark cheek-to-cheek smiles that made Julie grin right back. A hot guy on a motorbike with a ready smile like that? She doubted he'd be alone for long. Even with the gash and bruise on his cheek, he was something else.

"I'm sure, man," Tobin said. "The boat's been great — and Gramps was right about making us do it — but it's time for something else."

That seemed like her cue to speak up, so she did. "You're not leaving just to give us space, are you?"

"Hey, I just spent four months on a thirty-two-foot boat with my brother!" Tobin swung his arms like it was an amazing feat then patted the saddle of her motorcycle. "Besides, I think I got the good end of the deal."

Julie shook her head. She was definitely getting the better end of the trade: sailing with Seth instead of bumping around back roads on her own. Hard to believe her own luck.

It was crazy, how it all worked out. A whole twenty-four hours had gone by without her being chased, tied up, or shot at. She and Seth had made it back from the convent without a hitch and found Tobin just where they knew he'd be: on a stool in the very beach bar where they'd first met. A very hurried drink later — because who knew how long Sister Christine's tea and prayers could hold Leeds and Hernandez — they made a snap decision. Tobin would take the motorcycle and drive south to Pueblita while Julie and Seth grabbed a cab back to *Serendipity's* secret cove and set sail. They set a rendezvous for the same night in Pueblita, where they slept on it for one night. As Seth said, it was hard to make a reasonable decision after a near all-nighter.

Not that she and Seth got much sleep their first night together, alone on *Serendipity.* She was riding too big an adrenaline high, and the thought of having her very own pirate to herself was too good to resist. Their first time was fast and furious in the cockpit, folded around each other on one of the seats. The second time was slow and sweet on the comfy mattress of the forward cabin. And the third time? Sheer magic, the sight of the full moon over her lover's back as they lay intertwined on the bow of the boat, under the stars. And yes, he'd held her gaze the whole time, watching her come completely undone then following her right over the edge. She'd held on to Seth a long time after that, and it had nothing to do with the gentle rocking of the boat.

Now they were gathered on shore again, the three of them, saying their goodbyes.

"I figure I'll make Panama in no time on this puppy," Tobin said, running a hand over the motorcycle's tank.

"Lucy," Julie said. "The bike is named Lucy."

Tobin threw back his head and laughed. "I thought only guys named their bikes after girls."

"You're right. The guy I bought her from named her Lucy. Said it would be bad luck to change the name."

"Like a boat," Seth said.

Tobin gave a sly wink. "Well, I think Lucy and I are in for a lot of luck. And you two, too."

Julie went warm all over again. She and Seth were getting the chance she never thought they'd have. The chance to spend more than just a rushed couple of days together. And after that... For all that she tried not to get ahead of herself, it was hard not to imagine more. A lot more, for a good, long time. A lifetime.

"Just make sure you actually get some work done on your thesis." Tobin winked.

"Thesis? What thesis?" she joked. But yeah, he was right. Originally, she'd been planning to go home and work on her thesis for the next few months. But she could do that just as well from the boat, and the little bit of grant money she had left would stretch further in Central America than it would back home. They might even squeeze a couple of months out of it. Who knew? Seth had enough savings, too, for him to extend this dream just a little longer before heading back to real life and real jobs. In the meantime, they'd live the dream. Palms, islands, sunsets. God, life could be good.

"Are you sure you're sure?" Seth aimed the question at her this time.

She turned to see his brow folded in worry. Did he really think she could doubt him now? Did he really think she'd ever leave him? Okay, the whole steady relationship thing was uncharted territory as far as she was concerned, but she'd never felt more sure in her life.

She ran a finger along his jaw. "Your problem's gonna be getting rid of me, pirate, not the other way around."

He pulled her into the fifth spontaneous hug in the last hour. "Not a problem, Julie." He ran a hand over her hair as if to assure himself she was for real then murmured again. "Not a problem."

She could have stayed there forever, but it was time to get moving. The next adventure called: a couple of days' passage to as far into Honduras they could make it, and Tobin had to get going, too. The sooner they all got out of Belize, the better. Just in case.

"Hey, who knows," Tobin said as Seth pulled him into a back-patting man-hug. "We might meet up in Panama."

"Yeah, who knows," Seth replied, his voice breaking just a little on the words.

They broke the hug but stood eye to eye for a moment. It was another one of those moments that could never be captured on film, because that much emotion — brotherly love, a little worry, and newfound respect — was hard to squeeze into a lens.

Julie watched them, imprinting the moment onto her memory. She had the feeling she'd be doing a lot of that in the next couple of months.

Then Tobin pulled her in, too, and it became a three-way team hug, and that was even better.

"Be careful, man." Seth sniffed a little, squeezing his brother's shoulder.

"Don't tell Mom about the motorcycle." Tobin winked, then pointed a finger at Julie. "And you, no more package deliveries."

"Never." That lesson, she'd learned.

Tobin slid onto the motorcycle seat like he'd been doing it all his life and kicked the engine to life. He flashed another smile, lifted two fingers from the handlebar in a salute, and took off down the road.

Seth swung an arm over Julie's shoulders and pulled her close as they watched Tobin go. She could feel his chest rise in a sigh.

"Watch out, *chicas*," she said, only half joking. "He'll leave a trail of brokenhearted women from here to Colombia, for sure."

Seth tapped his fingers on her arm. "I'm not so sure. He packed that book."

"Which book?"

"The one with the picture stuck in it. Him and Cara."

She watched the trail of dust left in Tobin's wake and considered. "Maybe it's easier to break other people's hearts when your own is hurt."

"Maybe," Seth sighed. "Funny how it never hurt to see him go before." He shook his head at his own words then pulled her to his chest. "But this more than makes up for it."

She hid a smile in his shirt. "This?"

"You. Me. Us. This."

The sound of the motorcycle faded and the swishing sound of the waves filled back in. It was her turn to sigh. "Come on, sailor, let's get moving."

"You're sure you're good with an offshore trip?"

"I think I can trust my captain."

He blushed a little. A pink pirate. She liked that look on him, so she went on. "As long as we end up on our own tropical island somewhere. I owe you a night of missionary style on the beach."

"In the moonlight," he nodded, and his grin grew. "Think I forgot?" His fingers ran lightly up her arm. "I know exactly where I'm starting."

She raised an eyebrow, pretending she wasn't going all warm between the legs. "Where?"

He leaned in and ran a finger, featherlight, down her neck. "Can't give away the whole fantasy at once, you know."

She tightened her grip on his shirt. "Maybe just a little hint?"

Seth brushed his lips over her skin just above the hollow by her collarbone. "Right here," he whispered, working his way up to her ear. "I know exactly where I'm starting, where we finish, and everything in between."

"Seth," she murmured, running her hands over his firm rear.

"Hmmm?" It wasn't a question or an answer, just a supremely satisfied sound.

His breath was soft and minty on her throat, and it took everything she had not to throw him to the sand and shag him silly right there.

He pulled back as slow and reluctant as a man waking from a very good dream and looked around. "I guess here is not the place. We ought to get going."

She sighed. "I guess the lady selling bananas over there doesn't approve of this much heavy petting."

"So let's go." Seth led her down the beach to the dinghy, the two of them snuggled side to side.

"Where to, exactly?"

Seth threw an arm out over the view: an open horizon marked with stripes of green, turquoise, and brilliant blue. "Uncharted waters, honey. But somewhere out there is another Cayo Coco, waiting for us." He leaned in to her ear, his voice was low and gritty. "And the minute we get there, we're staying a week doing nothing but each other."

She hid her blush with a laugh. The straitlaced business guy had truly gone buccaneer.

"It's a date," she joked, then wished she hadn't. They'd parted two months ago with those very words.

Seth pulled to a sudden halt and fixed her in the eye with a look so earnest, it melted her. "It's not a date," he whispered. "It's a promise."

A note from the author

While Belize really does have a number of quiet beachside towns, Santa Marta and the Coco Loco Cafe are fictional places I created by combining the best (and worst) elements of real life. Likewise, Cayo Coco is a product of my imagination, but you'll find a hundred islets just like it off the coast of Belize. I have to admit to transplanting the beautiful colonial era convent from Guatemala, but Sister Christine is based on a real-life nun, right down her the brassy New York ways!

Sneak Peek: Entangled

Cara Leoni hasn't hiked into a mountaintop village in Central America to experience the rain forest; she came to seal a business deal. Everything depends on it – her job, her future, her pride. The catch? Her competition has already negotiated its own arrangement with the local chief. Now she's trapped in the jungle, the clock is ticking, and her only hope is the one man she vowed never to trust again.

Tobin Cooper was only planning on a couple of laid-back weeks on the beaches of Panama, but before he knows it, he's racing his rusty motorcycle into the wild side. Venomous snakes, poison darts, and ruthless drug runners aren't half as frightening as the idea of facing his ex-fiancée again. The odds of an epic fail are ninety-nine to one, but hell, his whole life had been lived in that one percent zone. But this time, it's not about adventure — it's about survival. If he and Cara are going to escape the jungle alive, they must rebuild trust, one kiss at a time.

Books by Anna Lowe

Serendipity Adventure Romance

Off the Charts

Uncharted

Entangled

Windswept

Adrift

Travel Romance

Veiled Fantasies

Island Fantasies

Spellbound in Sedona

Wind Whisperer (Book 1)

Fire Dancer (Book 2)

Dream Weaver (Book 3)

Sherwood Forest Shifters

Tempting the Sheriff (Book 1)

Tempting the Outlaw (Book 2)

Tempting the Maiden (Book 3)

Aloha Shifters - Jewels of the Heart

Lure of the Dragon (Book 1)

Lure of the Wolf (Book 2)

Lure of the Bear (Book 3)

Lure of the Tiger (Book 4)

Love of the Dragon (Book 5)

Lure of the Fox (Book 6)

Aloha Shifters - Pearls of Desire

Rebel Dragon (Book 1)

Rebel Bear (Book 2)

Rebel Lion (Book 3)

Rebel Wolf (Book 4)

Rebel Heart (A prequel to Book 5)

Rebel Alpha (Book 5)

Fire Maidens - Billionaires & Bodyguards

Fire Maidens: Paris (Book 1)

Fire Maidens: London (Book 2)

Fire Maidens: Rome (Book 3)

Fire Maidens: Portugal (Book 4)

Fire Maidens: Ireland (Book 5)

Fire Maidens: Scotland (Book 6)

Fire Maidens: Venice (Book 7)

Fire Maidens: Greece (Book 8)

Fire Maidens: Switzerland (Book 9)

The Wolves of Twin Moon Ranch

Desert Hunt (the Prequel)

Desert Moon (Book 1)

Desert Blood (Book 2)

Desert Fate (Book 3)

Desert Heart (Book 4)

Desert Rose (Book 5)

Desert Roots (Book 6)

Desert Destiny (Book 7)

Sasquatch Surprise (Book 8)

Desert Yule (a short story)

Desert Wolf: Complete Collection (Four short stories)

Blue Moon Saloon

Perfection (a short story prequel)

Damnation (Book 1)

Temptation (Book 2)

Redemption (Book 3)

Salvation (Book 4)

Deception (Book 5)

Celebration (a holiday treat)

Shifters in Vegas

Paranormal romance with a zany twist

Gambling on Trouble

Gambling on Her Dragon

Gambling on Her Bear

Gambling on Her Panther

www.annalowebooks.com

About the Author

USA Today and Amazon bestselling author Anna Lowe loves putting the "hero" back into heroine and letting location ignite a passionate romance. She likes a heroine who is independent, intelligent, and imperfect – a woman who is doing just fine on her own. But give the heroine a good man – not to mention a chance to overcome her own inhibitions – and she'll never turn down the chance for adventure, nor shy away from danger.

Anna loves dogs, sports, and travel – and letting those inspire her fiction. On any given weekend, you might find her hiking in the mountains or hunched over her laptop, working on her latest story. Either way, the day will end with a chunk of dark chocolate and a good read.

Visit AnnaLoweBooks.com